Love Over Lust

How Love Overcame the
Power of Addiction
A True Story

Karen Valiant

Writer's Showcase presented by *Writer's Digest*
San Jose New York Lincoln Shanghai

Copyright © 2020 by Karen Valiant

All rights reserved. No part of this publication may be reproduced, distributed, or transmitted in any form or by any means, including photocopying, recording, or other electronic or mechanical methods, without the prior written permission of the publisher, except in the case brief quotations embodied in critical reviews and other noncommercial uses permitted by copyright law.

ISBN: 978-1-953048-85-1 (Paperback)

The views expressed in this book are solely those of the author and do not necessarily reflect the views of the publisher, and the publisher hereby disclaims any responsibility for them.

Writers' Branding
1800-608-6550
www.writersbranding.com
orders@writersbranding.com

Contents

Introduction	v
Dedication	vii
Prologue	ix
TRUST	x
Part I: Now I Understand	1
It's All About Love	2
Love and Faith	5
Part II: Living the Lie	7
Chronicled Events	8
Beginning the Journey	20
The Woman	22
The Man	24
The Dream	26
The Adjustment	27
Warning Signs	29
Compromises	33
Betrayal and Deception	35
Part III: Truth and Recovery	37
Facing the Truth	38
Confrontation	41
Shock	43
Discovery	45
Feelings	47
Three Months Later	52
Treatment	56
The Battle of Good vs. Evil	57
Dealings	60
Organized Immorality	62
So Now the Paranoia is Setting In	66
Triggers	67
Who Is to Blame Anyway?	69
Your Own Friends and Family	71
Forgiveness	73
Victimization	75

Overcoming the Pain	76
Recovery of the Couple	78
Nine Months Later	80
The Future	83
Postscript	85
Epilogue: 20 Years Later	88
APPENDICES	91
APPENDIX 1	92
APPENDIX 2	94
APPENDIX 3	96
APPENDIX 4	98
APPENDIX 5	100
APPENDIX 6	102
APPENDIX 7	104
APPENDIX 8	106
APPENDIX 9	108
APPENDIX 10	111
References/Bibliography	114
End Notes	116

Introduction

This book was difficult to write. It was even more difficult to share the intimate details of our painful experience. Nonetheless we chose to revisit the events in order to enlighten the lives of others who may be experiencing a similar tragedy and to help others better understand the complex consequences of addictions.

We are taught that pain brings growth and understanding; that things happen "for a reason." We are told that good can come from bad life experiences. I am a living example of that wisdom.

What have I learned? Love is a precious gift that we freely choose to share with others. Love is unselfish. Love is forgiving. Love is pure. Love is a deep affection felt for another human being. Love, in action, is beautiful. It is the miracle that overcomes seemingly insurmountable obstacles.

Love sometimes involves a powerful sexual passion toward a special person in our lives. Lust also involves a powerful sexual passion toward someone else. In this one way, love and lust are very similar. Yet a vast difference exists between the sweet innocence of true love and the ruthless satisfaction demanded by lust.

Feeling lust is part of the human condition. Because lust is inherently selfish, it can become destructive. It may darken one's spirit. Sound, moral judgment discourages us from acting upon our lustful sexual impulses. Normally a person of sound mind and moral character can easily make an honorable decision, to disregard those sexual impulses. However, when a person has an addictive personality and is actively involved with chemical addiction, the chemical may impair that person's ability to make a wise choice. When a married person acts upon his/her lustful thoughts or feelings, he/she crosses a sacred boundary.

Unbridled lust is dangerous. Seemingly harmless curiosity with pornography can lead to sexual addiction. What may have begun as an intentional sexual stimulant becomes a consuming force that steals away one's conscience. Continued involvement with lust will leave only an empty shell of what was once a whole person. It replaces the unselfish natural love with an insatiable appetite for more selfish pleasure, at all costs. A person with an addictive personality can easily and quickly move from pornography to pornographic movies to strip joints and eventually to prostitutes. He/she becomes addicted to the lustful feelings and the false sense of power and adoration so readily available in our "sex for sale" businesses today.

When a person is driven by his/her hunger for lustful pleasures it becomes almost impossible to bring that person back to reality. We fight an extremely challenging battle to win back that person's soul. While the explosion of pornographic websites is alarming, lust is also aggressively promoted by every other form of media known to mankind.

Our story shows others how one man chose to enter the fantasy world of lustful living and almost destroyed the pure love in his life. It is the story of how one woman refused to give up, even when she had every reason to do just that. Love Over Lust is an example of the battle between Good and Evil and represents the hope we all have in the miraculous power of love.

Travel with me on this journey.

Know that you are not alone.

Believe that love can overcome lust.

Let the healing begin.

DEDICATION

This book is dedicated to my father who taught me wisdom, and to all the courageous couples who are recovering from sexual addiction.

Prologue

This book is a true account of two people who love each other. They were married for 14 years and had their share of trials and tribulations. Within three short months, their lives were shattered by the husband's multiple addictions. This book is written in an attempt to process, understand and help prevent similar events in their lives and the lives of others. For those couples who find themselves in a similar situation, hopefully this book will help begin the slow healing process. I have attempted to keep the text concise so that one might quickly obtain as much information as possible.

TRUST

Throughout our relationships,
One concept is a must:
Things can go much farther
If they're firmly based on trust.
Trust is something subtle-
It's an underlying theme.
It fortifies a world where things
Aren't always what they seem.
Trust is built up over time-
Its precious faith is learned.
Honesty applied to life
Is how this gift is earned.
Trust assigns a higher weight
To every promise spoken.
It can build so much while there,
So little when it's broken.
Trust is that sure link between
The truth and what is heard.
Trust is simply how you back
The value of your word.

-Bruce B. Wilmer

Part I
Now I Understand

For better, for worse
For richer, for poorer
In sickness and in health
Till death do us part.

It's All About Love

Love at first sight. It was the kind of love that swept me off my feet. I'd never experienced such magnetism toward a man. When we first met, I nervously stuttered as I introduced myself to the handsome stranger. I found myself behaving like an excited teenager again, searching for any way to make contact with Mike just one more time. I fantasized about our first embrace and what it would be like to be with this man. I hungered for him.

Much to my surprise, Mike was experiencing similar feelings. We got to know each other over several months, as he and a partner were working on home improvement projects for me. The first time we accidentally touched, I swear I could feel an electric shock (an unusual event in the cold, damp environment of the Midwest.) Our love took us both by surprise. It was so powerful that it derailed both of our eleven year marriages. It energized me, breathing fresh life into my stale soul. It gave me the courage to end a long-expired relationship and it thrust me into a hopeful future.

As faithful and honest a person you'd ever want to meet, I destroyed my marriage for the love of Mike. I deeply hurt my adoring husband. I broke my wedding vows and, in the process, alienated my family and marital friends. With two small children, I risked our happiness and security. I no longer knew the stranger in my own mirror.

My husband forced me and our children out of our large, comfortable home. We left, and I never looked back. There was simply no doubt; this was the right thing to do. I chose to pursue the love of my life rather than compromising my happiness for the sake of marital duty. We relocated into a small townhome and began our scary journey into the unknown. As I look back upon those times, I marvel at the miraculous recovery that all of us made, given the obstacles we had to overcome. My first husband and I eventually divorced, and he has yet to forgive me for the pain I caused. Until the events of the past two years, I did not truly understand the depth of his pain or the impact of my betrayal. Now I clearly understand.

Mike courted me for about eighteen months, throughout the topsy turvy times that are generated by two simultaneous divorces that seemed to "surprise" everyone. We were on a mission to be together.

One risky part of this new adventure was Mike's admitted alcohol addiction. He was not drinking when we met and had been working a twelvestep* recovery for over a year. His decision to stop drinking was one of the problems in his first marriage, for his wife refused to stop her destructive drinking behaviors and did not support his commitment to do so. Their lifestyles collided. Mike's family was so happy about our relationship because they knew I was supportive of his clean and sober lifestyle. They were so thankful to have "the other" Mike back in their lives.

We got married. Yet while Mike's family joyfully celebrated our union in the park-like setting in the backyard of their home, neither my sisters or brothers nor my parents came to the wedding. My father was still enraged with me. His powerful influence paralyzed my family, preventing them from showing any kind of loving support, understanding or encouragement.

I stubbornly chose to loyally support our relationship while sacrificing many other meaningful ones. Our love created painful battles between us and my family. We invested untold amounts of time and emotional energy attempting to repair broken hearts, left in the wake of our storm's path. I defiantly defended Mike throughout all of these trials. Love saw us through some extremely challenging times; experiences not uncommon to persons in second marriages with children and ex-husbands or ex-wives and all the other baggage that we carry into our second marriages. Time eventually mellowed the raw emotions in my family. I continued to defend the "rightness" of our union and anyone who spent enough time with us couldn't help but see the goodness in our relationship. Gradually, over a period of years, Mike was accepted into my family circle.

Love helped us through the worst times. We also sought counseling; individual, couple and group support. In retrospect there was rarely a time that we were truly at peace. The love we first experienced was being attacked from all directions, by life's many stressors. About seven years into our marriage, something in Mike snapped. He sunk into a deep depression. Therapy and medication were necessary to help him recover. Throughout the turmoil, however, Mike still kept his resolve to stay away from alcohol.

After about ten years of sobriety, Mike abruptly proclaimed that he believed he could handle alcohol. He rationalized that beer caused the problems in the past so he should be alright drinking a little wine in a social setting. He thought the other causes included his lack of maturity and irresponsible behavior. Who was I to tell him whether or not he could drink? Although I remember feeling scared and a little anxious about his decision, I was also hopeful that he was right. It would be pleasant to occasionally have a drink with him; to have a normal social relationship instead of fearing his relationship with alcohol and feeling awkward when we were around others who were drinking.

A couple months later we had a party in our home. He overdid it; drinking himself into oblivion. This was my first warning that alcohol endangered our relationship. The next day he was extremely apologetic and ashamed of his behavior. Did that cause him to quit drinking or me to panic? No. Instead he decided that rum would be his alcohol of choice because he obviously could not handle wine. I naively believed that this might be true. Rum continued to be his drinking buddy for several more years. Mike responsibly drank very little and drank seldomly. I kept reassuring myself that, indeed, Mike could safely drink. Maybe he is *not* an alcoholic after all. I chose to ignore the warning and hope for the best.

Love and Faith

For much of our married life we dreamed about living in the Rocky Mountain area. Mike had already been relocated in Arizona for a few weeks, waiting for me to soon join him, when I experienced a lovely dream. Mike had only been gone for a month but I missed him so. I was coping with the stressful responsibilities of caring for my children, ending my fourteenth year of work at the local high school and trying to sell our home. I was taking care of every detail by myself in preparation for the big cross-country move. I remember how tired and anxious I felt as my head finally rested upon my pillow one night in early June. In that dream, I clearly heard a male voice reassure me that, "Karen, it's all about love." The voice was not my husband's; it seemed to be one sharing wisdom from God. I awoke from that dream feeling so peaceful.

In mid-June, our home still had not sold and I was experiencing a tremendous amount of pressure and indecision. I didn't want to resign my secure job before we sold our house. I had not yet been offered a job in Arizona. A couple who was shown our house seemed very enthusiastic the night before but the deal fell through at 8:00 that morning. I was so discouraged. What should I do? That dream I had had the other night reminded me how "It's all about love." By 9:00 a.m. I was overwhelmed with an urgent feeling that it was time to resign, whether or not the house was sold; my place was with Mike, the man I love. That day, I wrote in my journal, "I have made the decision to move anyway, even though the house isn't sold, because, Mike, I belong with you…and I have FAITH that this will work out!" I typed my letter of resignation and presented the letter to my principal. Less than three hours later I received a phone call from another couple. They were ready to present a contract to purchase our home; we successfully negotiated the contract. As I read my journal entries at that particular time in my life, I had never, ever been happier and more excited about our future together.

Little did I know that, at precisely the same period of time, my husband was quickly being consumed by alcohol and sexual addictions.

Karen Valiant

I clearly understand that the events in our lives that I will now describe exemplify the miracle of love; its strength to see us through, against all odds.

Part II
Living the Lie

Chronicled Events

The following are actual events. These are the only documented sexual behaviors that I discovered. I may never know about other indiscretions. One thing I learned is that a person may not truly know another person, even if they are married to one another for many years. We all have secret, hidden parts of our private lives that we choose not to share with our mate. When those secrets reach into the perverted or immoral realm, we work especially hard to see that they remain secret. When addictions are involved, the secret is almost always sure to disrupt lives, cause financial hardship and many, many lies and eventually becomes secret no more.

Feb. 4: Mike is at a trade show overnight, takes the guys out; tells me it is to a bar. Later I find out that it was a topless strip joint two blocks from his daughter's home. The lies begin. I wasn't surprised that the guys were going out. The part I never knew until many months later, was that it was more than "just a bar." The only way I discovered the deception was as I poured over charge card statements from the past two years of our lives, looking for evidence of any hidden behaviors. I could tell that this place was a strip joint because the amounts were identical to those which appeared on more recent statements; same amounts, different states. I didn't learn about the proximity to his daughter's house until two summers later, when I was visiting her and I drove right past the place. I was sickened at the thought that grown men would behave in such a way but I was sorely disappointed that my husband had eagerly participated in this activity only blocks away from his own offspring. She later told me how she would be so disgusted to see those "dirty old men" leaving the establishment and she wasn't quite sure how to assimilate the fact that her own father was one of them. I still wonder how many other times he went to strip joints without my knowledge. All those years of Wednesday night bowling league games and the "going out" afterward; where was he really going? I will never know.

Mar. 10: Mike has been brought into the sales office as an "inside salesman," and uses the office technology to get involved with internet pornography. (In retrospect, I suspect that he was into that at least several months before when we suddenly received e-mail offers from X-rated companies.) Mike revisits several porno sites and makes copies. He begins his own personal porno file, with several websites noted for future visits. He carefully hides the file inside another personal file, kept in our home.

Mike spent many, many hours in the basement level of our home, supposedly working in his office. I never once questioned whether or not he was working. I did wonder about the excessive number of hours he would stay down there. I suspected he needed time apart from me and the kids and he found comfort in his cave-like office. Everyone needs their special, private space, I reasoned. Now I wonder if his demotion at work had to do with his failing work ethic. He was finding it more and more difficult to stay focused on work, on our relationship, on everything. I would be embarrassed to meet up with his fellow office peers, now that I know what they knew about my husband. It is so humiliating.

May 15: Mike goes out with a group of people from his new job. He proceeds to get so drunk that he has to be driven home by someone else. While at the bar, he overhears men talking about a nude(not just topless) dancing cabaret. When Mike described this event to me, he emphasized the social part of it, letting me believe he was fitting into the peer group at his new job. He never even hinted at the fact that he got drunk. One of the most significant parts of this night is the fact that his own mother was aware that he stayed out all night and he confided in her that he was so drunk he couldn't drive himself home. She chose to keep this important information from me, even as I later tearfully shared with her my suspicion that Mike was hiding the truth from me. I still have problems coping with her betrayal. I know now that she was simply being loyal to her son, but I wish I had known all the facts, early on, so that I had had a more complete understanding of the situation. I was trying to confront the problems while she was stuck in her old enabling pattern. How could I fight for us when I didn't even know what was the enemy?

May 20: Mike sees an ad for the nude dancing place in the local newspaper. I was not used to seeing XXX-rated ads in our local newspapers in the Chicago area. This still infuriates me, that our local paper insists on running these decadent ads. There is no concern for the persons tempted by sexual lust, the impact upon individuals and their loved ones or the responsibility for further destroying the moral fabric of humanity. I have tried, but failed, to influence the newspaper publishers to eliminate those ads. I will feel that my mission is accomplished when the newspapers no longer run the "sex for sale" ads.

May 25: Mike purchases an X-rated pornographic video from a local adult bookstore. He watches the video and makes his first visit to the nude dancing establishment that same night. He goes there alone. The cancerous seed has been planted, has rooted and is now sprouting. Even though I do not cherish the thought of any person frequenting one of these clubs, the fact that he went alone is very significant. If a group of adolescent-acting testosteronedriven immature males choose to go to a strip joint together, that is one thing (the group mentality.) However, the fact that he went alone tells me just how serious the situation already was. I was quickly losing my husband and there was nothing I could have done about it, especially being two thousand miles away from him.

May 26: Mike returns to the same nude dance club. When I saw this entry on the charge card statements, I thought I was going to vomit. Look at the frequency! The next night? I compared his behaviors to mine, at the same time frame. Here I was practically killing myself with all the work that goes into a cross-country move and he was frolicking around with naked women.

May 31: Mike returns. Not only does he return but now he is spending more money when he goes. This man is insane.

June 7: Mike returns. Funny. Now that I look at my journal entries, I see that he called me the next day. Was someone feeling a little guilty? Maybe there still is some small sense of conscience alive and working. I wrote about how adoring his daughter is, how sweet she was being to me, how I cannot wait to be with him on our new Arizona mattress. I even wrote about how attractive and handsome he is. Does this sound like a woman who is detached, cold, unloving, not meeting her husband's needs? I ask because that is exactly what people think when they hear about men or women betraying their partner. It is so unfair for people to judge others, especially if they have not walked in their shoes.

June 11: Mike returns. This is the day we sold our home. This is the same day that I made the leap of faith and decided to resign my job. I felt compelled to be with my husband because I thought he was the love of my life. Such an irony. There were also tornado watches all around me in my Illinois home. I would have much rather experienced a natural tornado than the storm awaiting me.

June 13: Mike returns. Mike leaves a very somber phone message for me. I journalled about how confused I was; how could he leave such a serious message when we had such good news in our lives? There was absolutely no excitement in his tone of voice. His spirit was dying.

June 14: Mike returns. On this day, I was writing about how close to Nature I was becoming. With the extra "alone" time I had, I would fill that time with bike rides and nature walks. I was sharing the excitement of seeing deer while riding. Mike would never feel comfortable sharing with me the details of his evening. Our lives were in total contrast.

June 17-22: I fly out to visit with Mike and I return to the Midwest on the 22nd. He was attentive. We were deliriously happy to be together. He showed me around his workplace and proudly introduced me to everyone. The sexual intimacy was remarkable. He was like a new man, totally energized. Now that I know what I know, I realize that he was at the height of his manic phase. I did secretly question how he got so good at love-making. I thought, of course, that he missed me so much that he became the world's most responsive lover. Now I discount those times because I realize it was not really Mike making love and I was simply a female body to him. He was acting out his fantasies which his nude girlfriends had created. I meant nothing to him at that time.

June 24: Mike spends over $1,000 at the same dance club. How about that? I am gone all of two days and he spends the most money yet. He had sunk so low into the sinkhole of insanity that he had lost touch with reality. Here we are, preparing to purchase a custom home and fully aware that our salaries are going to be significantly lowered, and he chooses to waste away over $1,000. I am totally unaware of the deception.

June 27: Mike returns. The pattern is set now. I am out of the picture and he is free to behave any way he chooses.

June 29: Mike returns. The establishments know him as a regular patron by now. He has shared his name, his workplace, his home phone number. They know his credit card number practically by heart. My husband is now a dirty old man.

July 2: Mike returns. This happens just days before we are to be reunited. Couldn't he wait?

July 3: Mike returns. I guess he just had to see her/them one last time before he figured his freedom was over.

July 4-9: Mike flies back to see me and pack for our move. Our closest friends host an awesome going-away party for us. I now join him for the road trip back. We are finally back together again.

July 17: We have an argument about his work schedule and his changed attitudes toward alcohol. Mike storms out and ends up at the nude dance club. I was tempted to follow him out the door but I stood my ground. I was determined not to stroke his ego by stooping that low. If he chose to act like an adolescent, he could do it alone.

July 18: Mike returns. How does he continue to cover up his secret life? I was living with him full-time in a one-bedroom apartment where we practically can hear each other breathe and he managed to keep me unaware. What a masterful liar! He, over and over again, returned to his girlfriends. It was no wonder that I felt so confused. He accused me of making him feel guilty over his work hours. Yet he distanced me as much as possible, covering up his actions with the lies about his work schedule. I was stupid enough to believe him, that is, until I discovered the lipstick smudged upon his collar. Now the truth was beginning to emerge.

July 24: Mike returns. I was being scolded, told to deal with his long hours at work or split up with him. I just looked at him as if he had gone mad. I am extremely worried about where he is headed with his disturbing relationship with alcohol; never once considering that there were other troublesome relationships in the way of our happiness. In my journal, I write, "It's as if the more confident he becomes with himself and work, the more careless he becomes with his body." I should have written, "It's as if the more involved he becomes with himself and his addictions, the more careless he becomes with his soul."

July 28: I am out of town for three days. Mike returns to the nude dance club. I remember phoning him from my daughter's campus orientation. It was late and he wasn't home. I called again. This time he answered, his voice sounding thick and muddled. I asked him if he were sleeping. He said "No, I must have been taking a shower when you first called." Strange, I thought, that a shower would make him sound so groggy. Now my intuition is telling me to question everything, but question it silently so he doesn't know that I am suspicious. I make a mental note to become more aware of his every move. Who is being secretive now?

July 30: Mike returns. This was his last opportunity to enjoy his girls, in my absence. My daughter and I had a pleasant, carefree time in Los Angeles. It was so much fun that I was ambivalent about returning to the stress of my marital relationship. My sister and I had a chance for a long talk and together we conclude that counseling may be a necessary step, to help save my marriage or at least save my own sanity.

Aug. 4: Mike says he is working late because of store inventory. Again, I believe the lie, without any suspicion. Having worked in retail myself, I rationalized that, of course he is doing inventory and that takes a huge number of extra hours to complete. I am trying desperately to be a good wife, more understanding. Mike returns to the dance club after quickly completing his portion of the inventory.

Aug. 20: Mike returns, follows the nude dancer to two places. When I saw the evidence of these actions, I went ballistic. Not only had the addiction drawn him back into the disgusting establishment but he obviously followed someone from one place to another. He must be having an affair. Or he had become a stalker. I was devastated. I was even more scared. I must admit that even though I have been using the words "sexual addiction," I still, at this point, had not equated that phrase to my husband's behaviors. My awareness went only as far as a very narrow definition of sex addicts, considering them only to be sex offenders. No, my husband was simply stressed out. That is all the understanding I could bear to grasp.

Aug. 26: Mike returns for the last time. This visit must have been very short. He certainly spent less money than usual. Something significant must have happened to him this day. On this day, I believe the spell was broken.

Sep. 20: I discover his secret life. In less than eight months, our lives are shattered by lies and addictions.

> Poem
> I came to explore the wreck.
> The words are purposes.
> The words are maps.
> I came to see the damage that was done and the treasures that prevail.
> Arienne Rich, Diving into the Wreck

Sep. 21:
"Hello. Is this Dr. Smith's office? This is Karen. I need to be tested for STD's (sexually transmitted diseases). When is the soonest you can get me in?...Yes, of course I will be there tomorrow, 1:00. Thank-you."

If you are reading this book because a similar string of events have happened in your life, the very first thing you need to do is to make sure you are both free of sexually transmitted diseases. Perhaps the most humiliating time in my life was while I was waiting in the doctor's office, to get my blood and urine screened. I didn't know whether or not I should have given them my actual name. If I do, will my employer figure out what is happening in my life? Will I possibly lose my job? Look how these people are treating me...they must know, they must know. Who will see my medical records? Does anyone here recognize me? How will we pay for all of this?

I was absolutely convinced that my husband had had sexual relations with at least one prostitute, so I felt it imperative to check out my health. My husband did not go in for testing and said there was no need because he did not have sex with anyone except me. Yet what did his word mean to me anymore? Nothing. The trust had been completely broken.

Sep. 28: "Hello, Dave? You don't know me but my pastor's wife told me you might be able to help me. My husband's gotten himself into big trouble with alcohol and strip joints. I don't know what to do!"

Our pastor's sermon included a reference to AA*. I hadn't even thought about that wonderful resource until then. A week later and my brain was finally starting to think again! The next several days I logged in many, many hours talking with a number of incredibly caring people who gave me tons of information and support. I quickly learned of local Alanon* groups, the area's addiction treatment programs and options, and I had an instant support group. I strongly urge any persons involved in similar circumstances to do the same. Local AA support groups can be located by calling an area pastor or hospital or mental health agency or by simply looking up "Alcoholics Anonymous" in the yellow pages. It wasn't until weeks later that I allowed myself to consider that my husband was also suffering from a sexual addiction and then searched for other appropriate 12-step support groups such as COSA*.

Nov. 15: "Hello. Is this Nancy Anderson, the lawyer? I'm calling because I have a tough situation. My husband has an addiction problem, has spent thousands of dollars in a very short time, and I am concerned about protecting our assets. What can or should I be doing?"

Most lawyers will offer a free one-time consultation. They do not charge for their services unless you hire them and continue using them for legal advice. So it was wise to contact a lawyer, especially since we had money that my husband could easily reach. In our case, we had a lot of money in both of our names at the bank, because we had just closed on the sale of one house and were waiting to purchase our next one. Either one of us could have removed all of it with only one signature. It was frightening. One's initial reaction under these circumstances may be to seek legal counsel regarding divorce. The lawyer can assist a person there, too, describing the general divorce legalities of your state of residence. I found that this was not the best time, however, to make any other life-altering

decisions because I had just entered a state of mourning. I was grieving[*] the death of an extremely important relationship-my marriage as I knew it.

Nov. 22: "Hello. My name is Karen. Is this the private investigator's office? I have a really bad situation here, where I cannot trust my husband and I need to go on a three day trip in January. Can you help me keep an eye on him while I am away?"

I never did go on that trip because I could not bring myself to leave Mike alone. I figured I would not enjoy myself, anyway, worrying about whom he was with and what he was doing. A private investigator is a good resource, however, because he/she may be able to give you information about the reputation of the dance club. Some clubs are known for maintaining a more "classy" atmosphere, carefully drawing the boundary between entertainment and prostitution or sexual touching. Other massage parlors and/or dance clubs allow all sexual pleasures. The private investigator can also give you some very good ideas for tracking devices that can be used. I decided not to use a private investigator because it costs a lot of money for each hour of service and they need a retainer just like a lawyer. There was no guarantee that Mike was still seeing "the girls," or that the private investigator would catch him, if he was. I found a different way to get to the "truth," which I will share with you now.

truth: That which is true; a statement or belief that corresponds to the reality (definition according to the Funk & Wagnalls Standard Desk Dictionary, 1984 edition) Dec. 1:

"Hello. Is this Fidelifacts? I need my husband to take a lie detector test. Can you tell me more about that? How accurate are the results? How soon can you get him in there to complete one? May I please help develop the questions?"

The decision to use a polygrapher was the result of a phone counseling session with Dr. Douglas Weiss, a sexual addiction[6] recovery professional. Again, I used the yellow pages to locate a polygrapher, but it helped me to first speak with a private investigator and use his/her recommendation. They usually know who is trustworthy. He helped prepare me emotionally, to be ready to deal with the results and be able to believe those results, whatever they may be. It sounds strange, but whether the results are positive or negative, his experience was that usually the woman has a difficult time accepting them. I know that a lie detector test sounds extreme, but this truly was a major turning point for us. It at least put an end to the constant, sickening questions that popped into my brain. I will share those questions and results with you later.

I wrote the following letter, in response to the endless media bombardment that was happening at the time in regards to the Bill Clinton/Monica Lewinski case. I could not escape the topic. Every time I picked up a newspaper, magazine, or watched the news I heard someone talking about either President Clinton or his possible sexual addiction or about Monica or Hillary or their daughter, Chelsea. Coincidentally the Phoenix area was publicly dealing with the issue of local sex clubs. The city council was voting as to whether or not to disband them. There were many newscasts, editorials and articles detailing that situation and even videos on the news, showing the inside of such clubs. I guess I had just had enough of it. The following letter and my diary entry were the results of that time period.

12-13-98
Dear Hillary (Clinton),
You and I have several things in common. We were both raised in Illinois, and we are about the same age. We are intelligent, educated professional women with daughters in their first year of college at prestigious California universities. We believe in the dignity of women and actively support that belief. We both love our husbands and they love us. We view our husbands as basically good persons. Unfortunately, I suspect we are both married to sex addicts. Our husbands still believe that they were "faithful" to us because they did not have intercourse with another woman, but we all need to face the fact that they are sex addicts.

My hope for you and Bill is that the two of you will bravely face this addiction together. There is help for both of you. You can begin the journey by contacting **http://www.sexaddict.com7**.

God be with you.
Sincerely, Karen

Dec. 13,1998: An entry from my diary. This was written at a time that my feelings had moved beyond the initial outrage to feelings of extreme confusion and depression. This was only three months into my personal recovery.

76 degrees, sunny, clear blue sky

Sounds like a dream come true, right? This is what Mike and I had been working so hard to achieve ever since we were married 14 1/2 years ago. So why am I so depressed? Why can I find so little joy in this Christmas season?

I am sitting here at the apartment in Phoenix, the one we will soon be leaving…and I am ready to "explore the wreck" of my life.-I am married to an alcoholic sex addict.-I am alone on most of my days off, like today, with no time together in this marriage.-and, I am vulnerable. I have no more energy to put into this marriage. It has died, thanks to the behaviors of Mike.

I have tried a plethora of things-reading, praying, talking, and writing. I've tried attending Alanon meetings. Yet I cannot find serenity. I cannot resolve the distance between Mike's immoral actions and the core of my belief system. He involved himself with a nude dancer, wasted away over $15,000 of our hard-earned money, and totally dishonored our marriage vows and my womanhood. How am I truly supposed to handle all of this? What does it really mean?

Addictions, addictions, addictions. Somehow he thinks that by saying he is sorry and then blaming all his negative behaviors on these addictions, he absolves himself of all responsibility. That was "the other Mike." Well, isn't "the other Mike" the one and the same Mike to whom I'm married? Is he a dual personality or what?

All I know right now, at this very moment, is that I am very tired of this world. I just want to finish writing this book and if that is why I am here, then I am done with God's purpose for me. God, please just take me away from this evil, sick, twisted place. So, God, please guide me through the writing of this book and do with me as you please.

Karen

Nine months into my recovery, I remained sensitized to any media coverage about male sexual attitudes. I wrote the following letter in response to a column that appeared in our local newspaper. I felt that the columnist presented a relatively unconcerned response about a very painful situation.

Karen Valiant

May 25, 1999

Dear Carolyn:

You just don't get it! Stag parties have become much more than a sexy girl popping out of a large cake! We are talking private body parts in men's mouths and vice versa; totally nude girls titillating their admirers. The "look but don't touch" rule doesn't exist at private parties nor does it exist at private rooms available at nude dancing clubs.

These "businesses" are organized to encourage immoral behavior and simply to make lots of money. The 18-year-old and older nude dancers are encouraged, taught, coached and urged to get closer to your boyfriend or fiance or husband or sibling or parent and develop a relationship so that the man will spend money to see them again; lots of money, to be with the "beautiful, sexy woman that adores" him.

"Boys will be boys" is just a stupid excuse that we naive females have allowed. Men want us to think that pornography, strip joints, nude dancers and stag parties are some sort of male right. "That's what men do." Men who continue to participate in these degrading animalistic behaviors do not deserve the company of a good woman.

Good men and good women of the world, it is time to make a choice between honoring women or the sleazy underworld. A man's true friends will stick by him, even if he has the courage to say no to these crude rituals and behaviors.

Speaking of rituals, past civilizations used to sacrifice women to the gods of fertility. Aren't we glad that someone put a stop to that one too? from "Wake Up!"

The following definitions, as recorded in the *Funk & Wagnalls Standard Desk Dictionary*, are included for a clearer understanding of sexual addiction: cheat: to mislead or delude; trick; to act dishonestly; to be sexually unfaithful dignity: quality of being excellent, worthy or honorable erotic: designed to arouse sexual desire exploit: to utilize for profitable ends fidelity: faithfulness to duties, obligations, vows gentleman: a courteous, considerate man honor: to bring respect or credit to or to dignify love: a deep devotion or affection for another person; a strong sexual passion for another person lust: sexual appetite or excessive sexual appetite; especially that seeking immediate or ruthless satisfaction; an overwhelming desire to have a passionate or inordinate desire, especially sexual desire moral:
   1. Of or related to conduct or character from the point of view of right and wrong: moral goodness.

2. Of good character; right or proper in behavior
3. Sexually virtuous; conduct or behavior with regard to right andwrong, especially in sexual matters obscene:

1. Offensive or abhorrent to prevailing concepts of morality ordecency; indecent; lewd.
2. Disgusting; loathsome; foul.

perversion: deviation from the normal in sexual desire or activities
pervert:
1. To turn to an improper use or purpose
2. To distort the meaning or intent or
3. To turn from approved opinions or conduct
4. To debase or corrupt; especially characterized by or practicing sexual perversion.

pornography: obscene literature or art trust: a confident reliance on the integrity, honesty, or justice of another; faith unfaithful: unworthy of trust; not true to marriage vows voyeurism: the act of sexual gratification by looking at sexual objects or acts

Beginning the Journey

My story will take you on a journey from false happiness to a reality of shock, sadness, hopelessness, frustration, and fear. Eventually healing, spirituality, and growth led to forgiveness. This is a story of a husband's hidden sexual addiction and his wife's struggle to cope.

For the sake of clarity, I will use the following definition of "sexual addiction:" a multifaceted addiction involving a biological component (chemical dependency/need for endorphins and enkephalins), a neurological conditioning component connected to an altered fantasy state, and psychological and environmental aspects such as physical, sexual and spiritual abuse and neglect, and real or imagined increased life stressors. The addiction cycle involves escalating repetition of risky, harmful, destructive acting out sexual behaviors in an attempt to escape pain or stress and in spite of the increasing loss and damage to real relationships. These definitions are described in the book, *The Final Freedom*, by Douglas Weiss, Ph.D. The chances of recovery, according to Dr. Weiss, are over 80%, if the person first is honest about what happened and then is willing to work on the recovery. Patrick Carnes, Ph.D., in the early 1980's, pioneered treatment and prevention of sexual addiction and compulsivity. He described the addiction cycle, in his book, *Out of the Shadows: Understanding Sexual Addiction*, as follows: an addictive experience which progresses through a four-step cycle and which intensifies with each repetition. According to Dr. Carnes, those steps are:

1. *Preoccupation*—the trance or mood wherein the addicts' minds are completely engrossed with thoughts of sex. This mental state creates an obsessive search for sex stimulation.
2. *Ritualization*—the addicts' own special routines which lead up to the sexual behavior. The ritual intensifies the preoccupation, adding arousal and excitement.
3. *Compulsive sexual behavior*—the actual sexual act, which is the end goal of the preoccupation and ritualization. Sexual addicts are unable to control or stop this behavior.

4. *Despair*—the feeling of utter hopelessness addicts have about their behavior and their powerlessness.

At the end of this cycle the addict feels such pain that he/she tries to numb those feelings with sexual preoccupation; thus re-engaging in the same cycle. Dr. Carnes goes on to explain that the addict suffers from impaired thinking, faulty belief systems and an increasingly unmanageable life. It usually takes a crisis to break through the self-destructive addiction cycle.

In his later book, Contrary to Love (1989), Dr. Carnes presents the Sexual Addiction Screening Test (SAST)*, to assist in the assessment of sexually compulsive or addictive behaviors. Although my husband still is unconvinced that he is a sex addict, I found the SAST screening test very helpful in my understanding of his condition.

The Woman

Let me introduce myself. My name is Karen and I am forty eight years old, relatively attractive and in good physical shape. I grew up in a large middle class family, in a small town in the Midwest. My family values honesty, hard work and education. I was raised by my natural parents and no other siblings have been divorced. I was married once before, which only made me more determined to make this second marriage work. A collegeeducated woman, I hold a well-paying, respectable job in an upscale community. I have donated thousands of hours of my time to drug/alcohol prevention programs with young adults. Awards adorn my desktop for leadership in prevention activities for youth.

I am a dedicated community member, belonging to the local church for several years. I am spiritually at peace with myself.

I also strongly believe in the dignity of women. I cannot stand to watch pornographic movies, and don't even feel comfortable with the Sports Illustrated Swimsuit calendar. I am sensitive to off-color jokes, "locker room" talk, and other forms of sexual harassment. I am the type of woman who is not afraid to contact my local newspaper upon discovering that it routinely published "Nude Female Dancers" ads in the sports pages and in the family entertainment guide. I have actively encouraged young women to work toward a non-gender biased world. I was involved in my union, to fight for wage fairness for women, reasonable maternity leaves of absence and other women's rights. The thought of men ogling and lusting over naked women sickens me. The realization that one of those men was my own husband is still almost too much to comprehend.

Mike and I raised two wonderful, bright, successful children who both attend prestigious colleges. The children had their difficult times with the complexities of divorced parents, stepparenting and the blended family concept. The family went through individual and family counseling, to help through the rough times, but at no time in the first fourteen years of marriage did Mike ever display behaviors that even hinted at a sexual addiction or problems with an alcohol addiction.

So you ask yourself, how can a woman like this get into a relationship with a sex addict with multiple addictions? How could an intelligent, educated, intuitive person make such bad choices? How could she even consider staying with her husband after discovering the painful, shameful truth about him?

The Man

Let's meet Mike. He is forty nine years old, intelligent, motivated, relatively handsome and in excellent physical shape. Mike also grew up in a large middle class home, raised by his two natural parents. His family however is riddled with addictive personalities and divorces. He loves sports and often enjoys bikeriding, hiking, swimming and skiing. He is high-school educated, took a couple college courses and holds a respectable management job. He earned outstanding salesman awards in two companies, as he led each of the businesses in sales for several years.

Mike attends church regularly. He became active in the men's church sports leagues and committee work. There are even times that he persuades me to attend church, on those summer Sundays that I would prefer to just sleep in and relax.

Mike has a twenty five year old daughter who adores him. Over a long period of time, she has also developed a loving relationship with me and my children.

Mike is my second husband. He had a past problem with alcohol and admitted that he used to "binge drink," but he had not had a drink for over a year before I met him. I respected him for his strength. One important detail he failed to tell me, however, was that on more than one occasion while bingeing, he ended up with a prostitute. Instead, before we were married, he told me that he had worked a 12-step program* for over a year. He was committed to keeping himself clean and sober, for his drinking had caused him many hardships: to lose his driver's license, his marriage and his selfrespect. He had worked hard to turn his life around. He portrayed himself as a tragic hero and a believable one at that. My husband, Mike, when he was not drinking, was charming, kind, and thoughtful. He was extremely fun and entertaining. I truly believed that people could change, and that my husband was one of them who that had done just that. I was so proud of him.

What kind of husband has he been? He has always shown me love and respect. He is relatively quiet and reserved but there is a playful adventurous side to him. He has a great sense of humor. He never forgets a birthday or anniversary celebration and carefully selects the perfect card for the occasion. Mike normally has great common sense. He willingly does his share of the household chores, balances the checkbook, and he attends to the loving, thoughtful details in daily life. He gives me physical love and affection, and genuinely enjoys many of the same activities as I do. He has never been much of a conversationalist though. He keeps a lot of his thoughts and feelings to himself. I need conversation so I fulfilled that need by creating a good circle of friends.

Over the years, Mike has experienced several bouts of depression. His issues include lack of self esteem, feelings of inferiority, lack of communication skills, and the frustrations inherent in a stepfamily and remarriage.

The Dream

My husband and I had always dreamed of moving to the West. In order to secure my divorce from my first husband, I literally had to agree to stay within fifty miles of him, (in the Midwest) because he had heard that we were planning to move out West. In a sense, we were in bondage to my ex until both of my children reached the age of eighteen.

Mike had helped raise my two children from the time they were ages three and five and now they were both finally in college. It was empty nest time for us! We spent eight years preparing for our move by planning multiple vacations to explore different parts of the Rocky Mountain Region. We settled upon Arizona, and it was nearing the time for us to begin our long-awaited journey. In late March we vacationed to Arizona one last time and found the perfect acre of land to build our dream home. We put money down, to begin its construction.

My work contract required me to stay until the summer and Mike's job was changing. In early Spring, he had been pulled "into the office" because his boss was redefining the role of the salespeople. Mike's salary was reduced significantly with the changes, so it seemed the time had come for Mike to move out West, ahead of me. I stayed back East, to handle the sale of the home, sale of my daughter's car, packing and all the other myriad of details involved in the closing out of our life in the Midwest. We were both so excited about our future.

Mike cashed out a small nestegg of funds and began the journey without me. He settled in Phoenix, AZ in late April. Mike found a small apartment, found a sales job and, alone, he began our new life. My plan was to move out to be with him as soon as the moving details were finished.

Our home sold quickly. I journeyed to Arizona in mid-June, to visit Mike and continue seeking employment. I interviewed at three places and was offered a job. The fates seemed to be with us; so many details were just "falling into place."

The Adjustment

I don't know how many of you have moved halfway across the country, but it is a very different experience compared to moving a relatively short distance or within the same state. It is extremely stressful, getting adjusted to unfamiliar streets, a seemingly foreign culture, an apartment versus the comforts of a home, and all new people. One experiences the loss of the network of family and friends and the comfort of knowing your way around. One must also go through the tedious tasks of changes of address, changes of license plates, finding new places to shop, do laundry and dry-cleaning, etc. etc. etc. Money seems to fly out the window with all the temporarily increased expenses. Moving from one climate to a very different one definitely offered its own set of challenges. The most difficult changes for me, however, were the alienation from my wonderful circle of friends and getting used to the recently emptied nest.

    By the time I settled in Phoenix permanently, Mike had already been there for almost three months. He had forgotten the first few weeks of his life out here, when he spoke of how he "may have made a mistake and perhaps he should just come back." "No…no…are you crazy?" I replied. "You are living our dream and I am so envious of you. Just give it some time and you'll see. I'll be out there soon. Hang in there. You will be just fine," I coached him. Well, I thought my coaching must have worked because, two months later, he told me he was "the happiest he has ever been." He felt like a "new man, born again."

    The first week of my living in my new 650 square foot home, Mike had to work an ungodly number of hours. He must have logged in over 100 work hours, while I sat at home or spent my time getting lost as I drove blindly from unfamiliar location to location. I tried to keep the apartment clean and I tried to prepare some decent meals for him, practically starving myself with the new time zone while waiting to eat with him when he returned from work. The Phoenix temperatures were hovering around 117 degrees…I thought I was in Hell!

Karen Valiant

Needless to say, I was not especially happy (who would be?) and I was experiencing culture shock those first few weeks. Mike could not understand why I wasn't ecstatic. We both knew that things would probably improve when I began my new job, because I was anxious to meet new people.

Warning Signs

I suspected nothing prior to our separation. Our friends had a wonderful going away party for us just before we left to drive out West together. It felt like a bridal reception, complete with flowers, cake, photographs, and gifts. We appeared quite the happy, loving couple to everyone there, and I felt happier than I have ever felt in my whole life. I still had no idea that my world would soon crumble.

Once we arrived in Phoenix, I cried many tears. Those first few weeks, I desperately missed my friends, family and familiar surroundings. I received little empathy from my husband (my first warning sign). Instead I noticed that Mike seemed hypercritical of every minute thing I did or did not do (my second warning sign). For example, he claimed that I left too many lights on and then he would complain that I turned off the wrong light. I made too much noise. I talked on the phone too much. I was not supportive enough of his job and how hard he was working to make our dreams come true. I was too demanding with his time. I should lose ten pounds (he had lost over twenty five pounds…another warning sign). I should be happier.

Mike was also physically unavailable to me. He was putting in extremely long work hours (so I thought) and was exhausted. I voiced my disappointment that he never once made an effort to come home to have lunch with me. After all, he only worked six minutes from our apartment. My mention of this caused him to fly into a tirade. He still continued to leave early, stay late and never came home for lunch. He was emotionally distant from me, as if his mind was somewhere else. I knew that he rarely enjoyed conversation, but I could not even get him to stay focused. He either had this vacant look in his eyes or rage.

I was also becoming aware of some disturbing drinking behaviors which had developed while we were apart those few weeks. He would come home and comment that he "needed a drink." Ordinarily, nothing would appear to be wrong with that comment. Yet remember that Mike has a history of alcohol-abuse problems. I did not argue with him about this because I remember learning that the spouse of an alcoholic can do more harm than good by trying to control the alcoholic. I had learned that it is his/her responsibility to take charge of their own life.

We had been going along smoothly with this new definition of his responsible relationship with alcohol, for five or six years, so who was I to question? I reasoned that maybe the "alcoholism as a disease" theory is, in fact, incorrect. My cohorts in the social work profession were convinced that there was no such thing as an "alcoholic" but in fact, that it was "irresponsible drinking behavior." I had even argued with a professor about the disease model vs. responsibility model. Maybe the professor was right because Mike was managing his drinking behaviors extremely well. We would drink occasionally (once or twice per month) and never to excess. Neither of us ever had more than two drinks apiece. The relatively new concept of **"needing a drink"** was scary to me. This was a different attitude. Mike would pour himself a drink almost daily that first week that I was with him. Just one.

By the eighth day, I began a conversation about my observations. I spoke about how I thought we were not going to be a couple that drank daily or after work to unwind. I reminded him that when we were together in the Midwest, we were occasional, social drinkers and that I did not think it was healthy for us to get into the habit of daily drinking. I told him that I thought it would be a good idea for him to stop drinking for awhile. Mike immediately got very defensive. He glared at me with eyes brimming with hate. I had never seen him like this before. My body tensed. He paced around the apartment like a wild animal. He called me a controlling bitch, among other things, exclaimed that he didn't have to "live like this" and stormed out of the apartment.

While I was taking a shower, he called from his car phone and left a phone message that said, "I love you, Karen. Listen carefully. I plan to spend my whole life with you, but you need to get a handle on your attitude toward my work hours. I am working my butt off, trying to make our dreams come true. If you cannot deal with the situation, then we should just call it quits. I don't know where I am going and I don't know when I will be back, but you think about what I am saying. I will talk with you tomorrow." **Who was this stranger? What is he talking about, "calling it quits?" Isn't this supposed to be the happiest time in our lives?**

He returned home that night around 12:30 a.m., wreaking of smoke and alcohol. I was disgusted. He was revolting. I asked him where he went and he cheerfully replied, "Just to that sports bar that Dave and I went to before. I just had a couple of drinks and now I am home!" I could barely sleep that night as I lay there frozen with fear.

The other addiction problem that I suspected was resurfacing was Mike's addiction to nicotine. While "back home" he had quit smoking six years ago; completely quit. I was so proud of him. I remember bragging about his strength as I worked with kids who were trying to quit the smoking habit, and I remember using him as an example to encourage them to quit. Mike and I had experienced my father's deterioration and death from cancer, directly related to his lifelong addiction to cigarettes. We had witnessed how my father tried but could not communicate through his tracheal breathing tube and how his own father had already been on oxygen for over five years because of lung damage from smoking. Mike's own father is now in a nursing home, dying from emphysema. We had both made a commitment to live healthier lives. Cigarettes were just not supposed to be a part of our lifestyle.

I remember the time that Mike flew into town, to help me do the final packing and to then drive the three day trip with me to our new home. When I gave him a hello kiss, I remember thinking that I tasted nicotine on his breath. I quickly denied that possibility, thinking that there was no way he would be smoking, after six years of freedom from nicotine and especially knowing how important it was to our relationship that he not smoke. Why would he do that on the day that I would be greeting him with kisses? No. It must have been my imagination.

We spent the next five days together, twenty four hours a day, getting ready for the move and then actually driving the distance together. Never once did Mike talk about smoking nor did I suspect he was sneaking cigarettes. But once we arrived here and he returned to work, I remember tasting and smelling that nicotine smell again, on his breath. I even confronted him a couple times and, looking me square in the eyes, he denied smoking.

It wasn't until we were on our way to our 14th anniversary celebration that I discovered the truth. Mike's parents wanted to treat us to an anniversary dinner. Because his father was connected to a traveling oxygen tank and needed to sit in the front of the car, I had to sit in the back of Mike's car. My foot bumped a metal box that was under the driver's seat and, being the curious person that I am, I opened the unfamiliar box. Much to my surprise, there lay a pack of Marlboro 100 Lights, Mike's favorite brand. I caught my breath. I could literally feel the blood draining from my face. I immediately wanted to bolt from the car. I thought I was going to be sick. Well, the rest of the evening was not very enjoyable, to say the least. Who was this stranger?! What else is he hiding? How am I to trust someone who lies straight to my face? What happened to the man that I knew back home? I had a thousand questions, doubts and fears. I again confronted Mike about his smoking, whispering to him that I had just discovered his cigarettes in his secret box. He could deny it no longer. That anniversary celebration was our worst.

Compromises

Remember the night that Mike had returned home from "the bar?" He had been drinking and smoking, but I rationalized that at least he did come back. Thus began the art of compromising myself and the situation. I convinced myself that since he came back, we must be okay.

The next day I was doing laundry and, just like a character in a movie, I discovered lipstick on the collar of his shirt from the night before. I confronted Mike about it and he very quickly replied that the "lipstick was nothing. There was just a bimbo pestering me at the bar, who wouldn't quit hanging on me as I tried to talk with another man there. It got so bad that the bartender made her leave, but it really was nothing." That was a reasonable explanation, I supposed. I didn't especially like the ease with which he described another woman as a "bimbo." I made a mental note of the disrespectful description and encouraged myself to listen for other signs of his different attitude toward women.

He of course apologized about the whole bar scene and walking out, and said that maybe I was right. He was willing to stop drinking and he would try to break the smoking habit. I pushed for him to do something different, this time rationalizing that the drinking was not out of control and I was more concerned with the health risks of his smoking. I asked him to please focus on breaking that habit. I figured that the sooner he stopped smoking, the better, before he got even more addicted to cigarettes. Thus I made another compromise which turned out to be a huge mistake.

Our lives continued along a strained but seemingly improving pattern. I began to come to terms with the concept of myself as a separate being from Mike. I began working on the idea of disassociating my feelings and my emotional reactions from his behaviors. I began really listening closely to words of songs and words of sermons. I was opening myself to change, for I had grown very tired of accounting for my husband's behaviors. I finally was letting go and internalizing that what he chooses to do with his life is between himself and God. I may not like what he does and I can let him know what is pleasing and what is displeasing, but he is the one who ultimately controls his own life. I was desperately seeking peace of mind.

Betrayal and Deception

The craziness continued. On one of his days off in late August, Mike left a message at my workplace. It said, "I found this great place to go offroading. I should be home before you get home from work. I love you." That message didn't surprise me since he had driven his 4-wheel drive vehicle off the beaten path before. I got home from work at the usual time. Two hours later, it was beginning to get dark and I still had not heard from him. I called his mother, who is in the area, and she had not heard from him either. I had this ominous, sinking feeling in the pit of my stomach. Mike was usually very dependable. We had formal house closing documents to be signed; ones that he had set out on the table for my signature.

It was already dark. He never showed. I ended up calling the sheriff's department and they began a formal search for him. I left a message on our answering machine, in case he called, and went to be with his mother, who by now was also extremely worried. We called emergency rooms, we worried even more, and we cried. We didn't know if he was seriously injured or dead. With temperatures reaching 108 degrees that day, we had reason to be concerned. Finally, at around 10:00 p.m., he called to say that he was fine, just very dehydrated because his car broke down in the desert. He had gone down too steep of a hill and when he hit bottom, the radiator hose had popped off the engine, leaving him stranded. He hadn't brought any water or phone with him. He said not to worry; he'd be home after they finished fixing the car. It would take about another 1 1/2 hours. I offered to drive out to be with him but he said that would not be necessary.

When Mike got home, he looked awful. He had taken a dip in the pool, to help cool off because he said he still felt extremely overheated from the dehydration. I stupidly offered him an alcoholic drink, which he sipped a couple times but said he wanted, instead, to take a cool, soothing bath to help him recover. He said he thought it better that he not have alcohol, with the possible dehydration. I spent the next hour or so bathing him and caring for him. When in bed I could smell the nicotine. Of course I had to comment on that, but I said I wasn't even going to allow myself

Karen Valiant

to react to it under the circumstances. He had been traumatized, after all, and the tow truck guy was smoking and it was too much of a temptation. Because we were up until 1:00 that night, I called in sick the next day. I was physically and emotionally exhausted. Mike, on the other hand, went to work, determined to keep the appearance of "normalcy."

Part III
Truth and Recovery

Facing the Truth

We began referring to the desert fiasco as "Desert Storm." Mike took a lot of grief over that, from the Sheriff's department to his work peers and family. He was extremely embarrassed about it and really did not want to discuss it with anyone. Over and over he admitted how stupid he had been, and I cannot count how many times I found myself saying that it was so unlike him because normally he is so cautious about the dangers of the wilderness.

But one thing didn't sit right: when I asked him how he got rescued, he said that two girls in their 20's came by in a jeep. They gave him water and let him use their cell phone. That was around 5:00p.m. So I asked, "If you had a cell phone to call the towing company, why didn't you make one more phone call, to let me know that you were okay?" He looked at me with a puzzled expression and replied, "I don't know. God, that was stupid of me! I guess all I wanted to do at that point was get out of the desert. I do remember that as soon as I got to the towing company, I was desperate to call you and I was so frustrated because I couldn't remember how to dial you, using the phone card with this new Arizona system." That conversation stayed with me, haunted me.

I called my sister, who is a counselor and one of my closest friends. We spoke about my observations and Mike's selfish, risk-taking behaviors. We both agreed that it wouldn't hurt for Mike and me to get back into counseling. The next day I announced to Mike that I thought we both needed to go see a counselor. I knew that my insurance benefits went into effect beginning September 1st and I felt I could benefit from some help dealing with my adjustment to Arizona. I also was looking for some help for him and his selfdestructive, narcissistic behaviors. He agreed to the counseling. We got an appointment for two weeks later.

The next two weeks were calmer; the quiet after "Desert Storm." I was beginning to feel almost normal again, whatever that was. The day of the counseling session, Mike called me to say he wouldn't be able to go because his mother needed him to help take his father to the doctor's.

I went anyway, alone. The counselor and I agreed that we needed to get Mike involved in counseling and we set up a second appointment.

The next two weeks were even calmer. We both went to the counselor for the next visit. I felt that Mike blamed me for all of our problems and described, as the key factor, my difficulty adjusting to this new environment. I was annoyed, for it appeared that the counselor was siding with him. I was given some irrelevant advice on how to try to stop controlling someone else. We set up a follow-up visit but hinted that we may even cancel it because things were going so much better between the two of us. That was on a Thursday. By the following Monday, all Hell had broken loose.

I had picked up the mail, as I often do. We had gotten a letter, some junk mail and a couple bills. One bill was a VISA bill, in Mike's name. I don't usually open his mail, yet this time was different. I was driven, I think, to look for the "Desert Storm" towing charges to validate that it truly happened the way my husband described. I decided to open this particular bill. I thought I was seeing things as I looked at the balance: $14,725! This must be a mistake, I thought. So I looked closer at the charges. My breath stopped as I saw, in plain print, "Dreamscape," $115.00, August 26th and "Entertainment Enterprises", $230.00, $230.00, $230.00…on what date?

The same date as "Desert Storm?" This really can't be happening! I looked closer at the statement, for any other questionable items and the rest made sense…$5000.00 that we used toward the house, when (June 10th?) the foundation was ready to be poured. Another $2,500 went toward our final payment of taxes back home, before the closing of our house out there. But there were thousands of dollars of unaccounted expenses.

I had just gotten off the phone with Mike minutes before I brought in the mail. We had been discussing how well things were going lately. I had commented how I thought we would make a good working team in a business and how I would like to talk some more about that after he got home that night. How quickly everything changed.

After discovering the shocking statement, I looked up the names of the two unknown items and found that they are listed under entertainment/nude dancers. I also looked into our business file to see if I could locate any other charge card statements. There were none. They had all been conveniently thrown away. So how does one get that kind of information? Oh, I know. You call the company that issues the card, tell them the social security number, the maiden name of the cardholder's mother and the birthdate of the cardholder, right? Sure, I had just done that with my own credit card because I needed to verify a specific payment. I didn't have Mike's social security number memorized so I went to the business file, thinking "Where would it most likely be? I know! His old Marine file. Uncle Sam must have had it."

Much to my surprise, there was a new-looking file folder placed into the back of that old, old Marine file. When I opened it (curiosity again) I almost fainted. there was a 30-page file of pornographic internet photos and a whole list of web addresses, in Mike's handwriting. I felt the color drain from my face and a cold emptiness surround me. I collapsed onto our bed and began sobbing deep soulful sounds of the brokenhearted. My daughter instantly ran into the room to console me. Life as I knew it was over.

Confrontation

There was no sense wasting another minute before confronting my husband, for I could barely breathe. I felt like someone had just "sucker punched" me in the stomach. My voice icily caught in my throat as I dialed his business number. My hands were shaking. The receptionist answered the phone call, pleasant as always. I asked for him, trying to use my most normal voice to avoid alarming her. Mike cheerfully answered the phone. "Mike?" I croaked, "I just opened your VISA statement and found some terrible things on it. Like a $15,000 balance and charges to nude dancing clubs…WHAT IS THIS?"

"Karen, it is not what you think."

"Mike, WHAT IS THIS?"

"Karen, we will talk about it when I get home."

"NO! We will talk about it NOW!" I screamed, barely recognizing the sound of my own voice.

"I can't. I'm at work. There are people around."

"I don't care about the other people. WHAT IS THIS?" I screamed, even louder this time.

"It is not what you think, Karen."

"What is it…prostitutes? Drugs? Gambling? All of the above?"

"No. It's not any of that. We'll talk when I get home." "Tell me now, damn it!" There was silence, then.

"It is a Cabaret. That's all. It was me being stupid. I can't say any more." I was speechless. After a brief silence I slammed the receiver down.

And I cried and cried and cried, uncontrollably. I hadn't even confronted him with the pornography yet.

Fortunately I had a place that I needed to be that night. I don't know to this day how I ever got through that community choir concert rehearsal, but I did. I was shaking so badly that my daughter had to drive me. I couldn't eat. I was so tense that I could barely force out the musical notes. I slumped into a chair in the corner of the last row, trying to participate (I guess to prove to myself that I was still alive) but wishing I could disappear and die.

When I arrived home that night, Mike was sitting on the sofa, waiting for me. I silently signaled to him that we needed to go for a walk. There is no way that I could have calmly sat still to confront issues of this magnitude. I also didn't want my daughter hearing what might come out of my mouth next because I had no idea of what I might say. For the next hour we walked (actually I paced and anxiously wrung my hands) and talked and I cried and screamed. He tried his best to explain what had happened. As we neared the apartment again, Mike said he loved me and he then tried to touch my hand. I recoiled from him, keeping my arms plastered to my sides. The thought of touching him sickened me. In the end we agreed that it would be best if he left our place and we had at least several days apart; time for me to sort through all of this. I especially did not want the pervert anywhere near my daughter. Mike left that same night.

To summarize, Mike's explanation is that I was right all along and that in fact he had gotten more involved with drinking. He had gone out with the guys one night, to a bar, and overheard a group of men talking about this stripper's club. The next day or so, while reading the sports section of the newspaper, he saw an ad for that same club and began making plans to go there alone. The evenings before his days off, he would go to different strip joints and stay until 2:00 a.m., drinking, smoking, and paying strippers to perform. He worked his way up to paying for "private shows" with one particular stripper. She even started calling him (soliciting) at his workplace. He claims, of course, that he did not have sex with her, but that he wasted thousands of dollars pleasuring himself with her and others. He had stopped going on his own, four days after "Desert Storm." As for the pornography, it meant nothing. It was just "men being men." A guy at work showed him the websites and he had made copies of pictures for himself. It is just a "guy thing." He was "just curious."

Mike was horrified that I found out about all this. If I wanted a divorce he would understand and would not fight me. He was willing to go back to counseling and deal with this situation. He promised to never frequent the strip joints and/or the nude dance clubs again. He will stop drinking immediately. He will work to quit smoking. He said he was willing to do anything to make it up to me.

Shock

My initial reaction was shock. It was as if my life had been hit by an earthquake, with a magnitude of ten! For almost a week, I completely lost my appetite. I would try to eat but food would just get stuck in my constricted throat. I was nauseous. I could barely breathe; I had to carefully force myself to take deep breaths to relax and be able to work. My heart was racing. I could not sleep more than two hours at a time, and I would always awake in tears.

Through it all I kept reporting to work. At least work could temporarily take my mind off this mess. Being a professional, I carefully attempted to leave my personal problems at home, but my mind drifted from the workplace to the homefront and back again thousands of times. I could not stand the thought of eating with any other staff members. I felt unworthy of human companionship. The idea of conversation frightened me. If only I could crawl into my safe, empty bed and hide. I was numb. I was scared. I could barely concentrate.

I remember calling back the therapist the day after Mike moved out, to inform him of the new developments. I first urged him to see Mike alone during the next visit. I reasoned that **Mike**, indeed, has the problem, not I, and that I would depend upon my wonderful family members and friends for support. Unfortunately I was so embarrassed and ashamed that I could not find the courage to call anybody. I called back the therapist, before Mike's scheduled appointment to ask if I, too, could see him; perhaps the two of us together for now and then separately later. The therapist agreed. He urged me to maintain my highest level of integrity during this difficult time. I wasn't quite sure what he was talking about because I had every intention of being faithful to my husband. At least one of us could do the morally "right" thing. The therapist also gave me some community resource phone numbers for Alanon and COSA.

While I was in this state of shock, I found myself doing strange things, like pulling up to the gas pump on the wrong side of it, or sitting through a green light or completely missing a familiar turn. I had to force myself to concentrate and had to be extra careful while operating a vehicle. I was a dangerous driver at this time. My mind was out of control. My heart was broken. Who cared about the "rules of the road"? I still have no idea how I was able to counsel others professionally at work when I myself was in such a desperate state.

Discovery

The next stage that I went through was that of wanting to know every little sordid detail about what happened. How did all of this begin? When was the first time? How often did Mike go to the strip joints? Which ones? How much did they strip off? (Oh, my God, they were nude!) When did he print the pornography? Why? Why? Why? How many clubs did he frequent? What was the pattern? How many strippers did he see? What exactly was going on at those private shows? Was there one in particular? What did she look like? What is her name? Where does she work? Did he ever let her into our car, our home? Did he ever get into her car? Did he try to call her? Did he meet with her outside of the dance club? Did she contact him at work? At home? Did he go to the dance club alone or with someone? How did he end up spending so much money? How did he expect to keep this a secret? How much did he have to drink? Were drugs involved? What exactly did the stripper do; touch his body? Rub her body against him? Did he touch her body? **What was he thinking?** How did he think I would feel, knowing what he was doing? What does he think about women? How unattractive am I for him to need to do this? Does he still love me? How can we survive this?

    The discovery stage of recovery lasts a long time. The questions come in waves. Sometimes I would wake up with a question gnawing at me or I might even dream of a question that I hadn't yet asked. ALL THE QUESTIONS HAD TO BE ASKED FOR ME TO MOVE FORWARD. I had to go back before I could proceed forward. In this particular situation I could not begin the healing process until all the questions were answered. I didn't have to accept or necessarily believe all the answers, but I did ask the questions and demanded answers. I figured that if my mate was sincerely interested in healing, he would cooperate with me. And he did. Yet never did he provide me with any more information than I requested. It became apparent to me that, no matter how humiliating or embarrassing the question, it needed to be asked. He certainly was not going to volunteer anything. I had nothing more to lose by asking.

When asked the big question, **"WHY?"**, Mike answered that he didn't know for sure. He believed he was just having some fun and could stop at any time. He reasoned that, as long as he did not have sex, he was still being faithful. What was wrong with a lonely man looking at flesh?

He thought his behavior had something to do with feeling like "the big man," and he felt powerful throwing all that money around. He enjoyed the attention he got. The women showered him with adoration and compliments. "His" special gal spent hours not only erotically dancing nude but she also would "just talk" with him. She would give him a special hug when he left. Mike thought of the girls as his new friends. Now that our money has stopped flowing into their hands, where are those "friends?" Why couldn't he feel satisfied to talk with me, his mate? Was this an affair? Why was our sexual intimacy the best it had ever been and that still wasn't enough? I know that I am certainly not the best dancer in the world but I believe I have been a good wife and partner.

Feelings

The following music helps describe my feelings of defiance and determination. I found that music was extremely important, and still is, in helping me find the words to express my feelings. This particular song was important to me during the first month or two of our crisis. I needed to detach myself from Mike. This music and these lyrics helped me continue the emotional separation process that is so important in the destruction of codependency.

You'll See, by Madonna, Copyright 1995 Maverick/Warner Brothers Records Inc.

> You'll see.
> You think that I can't live without your love.
> You'll see.
> You think I cannot go on another day.
> You think I have nothing without you by my side.
> You'll see, somehow, some way.
> You think after all you've done I'll never find by way back home.
> You'll see, somehow, someday.
>
> Chorus #1: All by myself, I don't need anyone at all.
> I know I'll survive.
> I know I'll stay alive.
> All on my own, I don't need anyone this time.
> It will be mine;
> Noone can take it from me.
> You'll see.
> You think that you are strong, but you are weak.
> You'll see.
> It takes more strength to cry, admit defeat.
> I have truth on my side.
> You only have deceit.

You'll see, somehow, someday.

Chorus #2: All by myself, I don't need anyone at all.
I know I'll survive.
I know I'll stay alive. I'll stand on my own.
I won't need anyone this time.
It will be mine.
No one can take it from me.
You'll see.
You'll see.
You'll see.

The next stage of healing is extremely powerful. It is the aftershock that follows the initial earthquake. This one is the feelings stage. This is when the shock wore off and all those (previously protected) feelings began pouring out of me. I felt a tremendous amount of confusion, guilt and outrage at first. There were lots of tears and anger as I experienced the shame and humiliation, the embarrassment, the feeling of being unattractive, feeling responsible, wanting to hurt my spouse, feeling betrayal in its rawest form, and disgust of the opposite sex.

I felt dirty. My husband had been consumed by lust. Mike was actively seeking a relationship with nude dancers. My husband had sought the company of women who would lower themselves to the filthiest level of existence. He allowed himself to be their prey. He became a "regular" patron of those sleazy, grimy, smoke-filled, drunken, low-life perverted places and had the audacity to feel comfortable there and fulfilled and happy. He had engaged in who-knows-what sexual behaviors while exploiting women, dishonoring me and ruining us financially. Their company was more important to him than our relationship. Women were simply objects to him; sexual toys. I did not want him to even touch me after all that! Yet he had touched me, intimately, for months, while I didn't know this secret life. I felt like his perverted activities dirtied him and he had passed the filth onto me. I remember literally needing to shower, to physically cleanse my body. Even several months later I felt the need to cleanse my soul. Yes, I felt dirty.

I felt an overwhelming urge to run away. Who needs this? It was just too much for me to handle. I wanted to move back home, where I could seek the security of my family and friends. But, no, how could I tell them?

How can I even put this shameful situation into words? How would they ever understand? Maybe I could stay with friends back home and get my old job back and—screw him—I'll make it on my own! Maybe I'll just keep going out West. My sister in California would help me get established. I could easily find a job and my daughter's tuition costs would be thousands of dollars less. Running away may be the best solution.

I blamed everyone and everything for the pain in my life. First and foremost I blamed Mike. I even fantasized about killing him. I am normally a non-violent person but I had been pushed over the edge. I can now better understand the motivation in crimes of passion. I am thankful we had no weapons in our home because I could have easily used one at this point. I also blamed Mike because of his irresponsible choices. He knew he had an alcohol addiction problem yet he chose to re-enter the drinking world. He knew that pornography was distasteful and upsetting to me yet he chose to involve himself with it. He definitely knew how I felt about fidelity, honesty and commitment yet he chose to break our vows. I not only blamed him but, at first, I hated him for what he had done to us.

Sometimes I began blaming other things or people such as our sick society or the media or Mike's family and their values. I blamed the sexually oriented newspaper ads. I, of course, blamed the nude dancers. What kind of women would devote themselves to the moral destruction of a man and contribute to destroying our marriage? What kind of women would exploit my husband? Can't they find any other respectable line of work? How could these women degrade themselves? What right do they have to steal my husband's soul? I almost visited one of the establishments, to confront the people there. Instead I parked my car across the street from one of Mike's favorite places and imagined him parking our car there, entering the sleazy place, being greeted by his new "friends" and then pleasuring himself with them. I never wish to go through that experience again. To this day, I avoid going anywhere near that place because it dredges up such painful emotions.

I continued to blame. I blamed my own family for not showing enough support for our marriage. I blamed the internet for marketing pornography and the adult bookstores for making pornographic materials so accessible. I blamed the government for failing to regulate pornography and sex clubs. I blamed Satan himself for using pornography and sex clubs to enter my husband like a hungry cancer and causing it eventually to kill our marriage after sucking the light out of Mike's soul.

I naturally blamed myself. Why did I ever allow Mike to begin drinking again? Why didn't I see what was happening? What could I have done differently? Why wasn't our relationship and my body more satisfying? What was I thinking, to marry a sexual pervert? Maybe he would be better off if I were gone.

I even went through a period of time that I blamed God. How could He let this happen? How could He do this to me? to us? What had I ever done to deserve such treatment? How strong does He think I am? I am not! Why would a loving God hurt me so? Why me?

There was so much anger that if I could have taken it and turned it into electricity, I could have lit up New York City for a week. My body and soul oozed anger. I hated what my spouse had done to me; to us. I could not help but relive the vision over and over and over again, of Mike betraying me with another woman. I could visualize his being pleasured by her. I have a very clear image of him sitting at a table in some dimly lit room, music blaring, Mike with a drink and cigarette and completely mesmerized by her erotic dancing. I can still visualize him touching her and her doing sexual things to and with him. I imagine him laughing at me and I can hear him sharing intimate details of our lives with that beautiful stranger, oftentimes complaining about my disappointing relationship with him. It doesn't matter how many times he denies having had sex with another woman, there will always, always be that fear that he did. I will never be able to trust him fully again…never.

How unfair this is! Here I am, a 48-year-old woman. I have taken excellent care of myself but there is no way that I can compete with the looks of those perfect bodies. Every time my husband makes a comparison, I will lose. Every time he enters his sexual fantasy world, I will lose. If he cannot change his behaviors, we both lose because I will leave and our marriage will be history.

There is a tremendous amount of sadness here too. I felt like I was grieving and, in fact, I was. A certain innocence was gone. Our old relationship had died. It will never be the same. I didn't feel married any longer. I felt like removing my wedding band and I did. I could not even imagine when I would feel good enough to put it back on again. I also felt guilty about all the grief I had caused my children because of Mike and his inability to love them. The stresses and strains caused by a stepfamily had taken their toll on all of us. I was so sorry that I had wasted fourteen years of our lives with him and that I forced him upon them. What must they think of me now? Will they ever forgive me?

I felt so betrayed. The lies, the secrets, and the indiscretions were all part of the package. There were times I even wished that he had had a "normal" affair rather than his chosen "abnormally" perverse, demeaning relationship. Anyone who knows me, sees me as a very honest person who believes in fidelity and commitment. Now I felt like I had an open wound created by the most significant person in my life.

I was feeling very much alone. Who can really understand what I am experiencing? How do I talk with my family without making them hate him? How do I talk with his family? How do I talk with my own children? How do I discuss this with my best friends without permanently affecting our relationship and perhaps even losing them as friends?

I also thought I must be the most unattractive woman alive. I know my beauty is fading as I age but I could lose a few pounds and firm up. Another man might help me feel sexually complete again. It was obvious that I was feeling extremely vulnerable. Now I know why the therapist first cautioned me to maintain my highest level of integrity. There were several times that I just wanted to grab the nearest male body for my own sexual pleasure and, of course, to spite my spouse. Thankfully I did not succumb to my own sexual impulses. Instead I have maintained a higher moral code of conduct throughout this journey. No matter how strongly I felt the lure of sweet revenge, I reasoned that two wrongs do not make a right.

Three Months Later

At about three months into my recovery, I was often overwhelmed by feelings of depression. I still cried daily, often sobbing. I had so much pain to process and each time that I cried I felt I had released one more small part of that pain. Eventually I grew very tired, both emotionally and physically exhausted. The following song expressed my need to be comforted and my search for peace.

Angel by Sarah McLachlan, copyright 1997, Arista Records Spend all your time waiting for that second chance; For a break that would make it okay. There's always some reason to feel not good enough, And it's hard at the end of the day. I need some distraction, oh a beautiful release. Memories seep from my veins. Then maybe empty or weightless, And maybe I'll find some peace tonight. Chorus: In the arms of the angel, Fly away from here. From this dark cold hotel room,

And the endlessness that you fear. We are pulled from the wreckage Of your silent reverie. You're in the arms of the angel. May you find some comfort here. So tired of the straight life, That everywhere you turn, There's vultures and thieves at your back. Storm keeps 'em twisting. Keep on building lies That you make up for all that you lack. Don't make no difference. Escape for the next time. It's easier to believe in this madness, Or this glorious sadness, That brings me to my knees. Chorus: In the arms of the angel, Fly away from here. From this dark cold hotel room, And the endlessness that you fear. We are pulled from the wreckage Of your silent reverie. You're in the arms of the angel. May you find some comfort here.

You're in the arms of the angel. May you find some comfort here.

I still had these gnawing feelings of hopelessness and fear. It didn't help the situation when I was receiving all sorts of strange phone calls, including "dating service calls," women asking for Mike, hang-ups, and untraceable calls. At one point, a woman called me, accusing me of having an affair with her husband because our phone number was on their phone bill several times. The only reasonable explanation for this was that perhaps one of the dancers worked with her husband or was a "friend" of his and she borrowed or stole his cellular phone to contact my husband. When I confronted her husband, he thought I was a private investigator or a bill collector. The explanation was not as important as the fact that I was now dealing with irate wives, accusations, and more situations from the "gutter life." It was madness.

I could not get past the painful image of my husband with another woman and I could not believe any of his words because, in fact, that is all they were to me now, just words. I was convinced that a person could not spend thousands of dollars and see the same woman many times without having sex with her. Mike's words were never to be trusted again for I came to realize that Mike is a very good liar.

With the house closing looming over my head, I needed to make a huge life decision: do I or don't I want to commit to a new life in a new home and large mortgage, with a man that I cannot ever completely trust again? I was still in so much pain. If only I could make this decision later!

I decided to look for answers from other professionals. I spent hours and hours combing through books, looking for some sort of direction. However multiple trips to the self-help section of bookstores failed to connect me with books about sexual addiction. I was too embarrassed to ask a bookstore clerk for help. While skimming through one of the self-help books, I did come across an internet website about sexual addiction. I wrote that particular address down: www.sexaddict.com, with the intent of exploring it in the privacy of my own home. This internet address began my healing process, because I finally found the people who could really understand and the information that could actually help. The website lists information, books, audio tapes, videotapes and other resources available.

I even had the opportunity to arrange a telephone counseling conference with one of the authors. It was during this phone conference that I was able to define that my husband, in fact, is a sex addict. I also explored the question of my future with this man. I was urged to face the big question: "Do I want to know the truth? Or do I want to live the American dream, in our beautiful new home, pretending that everything is okay, distracting ourselves from the problems at hand?" After I hung up the phone, I sat myself in front of a big mirror and asked myself that exact question. Do I want to know the truth?

The only way to begin to know the truth, the professional advised, was to have my husband take a lie detector test. This is standard practice that he uses in treatment of each sex addict. I would never have considered that option on my own; it seemed so cold and heartless. Yet it makes sense, to have a baseline of information and, finally, *TRUTH*. My life had been attacked by so many lies and deceptions that, as frightening at truth could be, at least it would be real.

I searched for the most reputable polygrapher in the area to set up the appointment. I then spoke with Mike about my need to have him do the lie detector test. He was angry! He spoke of the humiliation in having to do that but I insisted that the only way I could make a commitment toward our future and the house was for me to know what really went on between himself and his favorite nude dancer. I had already concluded that if he was lying about that (he claimed he never touched her) then we were finished. I desperately needed to begin our "new life" based upon honesty. However I also knew that I was risking the end of our marriage if/when it was confirmed that he had had intercourse with her and had continued to lie about that. So I took the risk, Mike took the test (four times, to be exact) and passed it. Here are the questions I developed. They were intermingled amongst others.

"During the past year, have you had intercourse with a woman outside of marriage?"

Answer: "No."

"Have you had more than one sexual partner in the past 5 years?"

Answer: "No."

"Has a woman, other than your wife, had oral sex with you?"

Answer: "No." "Have you touched another woman's breasts or genital area?"

Answer: "No."

I myself helped design the questions so that he could not wriggle his way out of anything. We had just jumped one huge hurdle!

So now what? What was going on, that a man could say he "felt the best he ever had," he spent all this money, wasted it away sitting next to a naked woman and watching her dance and didn't even try to have sex with her? I knew that we needed to look further for answers. It just didn't make sense. So

I continued to read and read and read. I consumed many books, quickly. I finally stumbled upon a lifesaving book, called *An Affair of the Mind,* by Laurie Hall. It is relatively long and has many Bible scriptures quoted throughout the book, but it is exactly what any woman in this situation needs. I highly recommend it for an in-depth understanding of what a woman may be feeling and experiencing. She shared almost identical thoughts, feelings and embarrassing moments that I had had. Her book covered a span of over twenty years of her husband's sex addiction and her eventual discovery of the problem. Our situation, however, took place in less than eight months.

I reasoned that there must be more happening here. My next reading included the DSM IV manual, a professional resource to help social workers, medical doctors and psychiatrists diagnose/define mental disorders. I copied several pages from that manual and brought them to our next counseling session. Thus began our next phase in recovery: treatment.

Treatment

What I believe we are dealing with, in my husband's case, are multiple addictions to alcohol and sex. The drinking triggered a manic episode[10,] or to be more accurate, a "substance-induced mood disorder". Mike was experiencing multiple stressors, with the move, a new job, new house, and being alone for the first time in our marriage. His father's health was failing and Mike was the primary source of support for his mother. When he went out to a bar with the group from work, he allowed himself to get very drunk and that behavior triggered the beginning of a manic phase.

All of the rest of Mike's behaviors were a continuing search for the "high" he experienced, pleasuring himself. His brain's pleasure center could not get enough. What I observed as "narcissistic behavior" was the result. For a clearer understanding of "compulsive pleasure seeking" behaviors, I highly recommend the book, *Craving for Ecstasy*, by Harvey Milkman and Stanley Sunderwirth. Mike was caught up in an endless loop of drinking to relax, then lowered inhibitions because of the drinking, and an increased craving for the ecstasy that all of his addictions provided.

Mike, through months of counseling, was also able to trace a family history of manic/depression and was able to deal with his feelings of emptiness, following the suicide death of his brother only two years before. The counselor referred him for a psychiatric evaluation and he is now on a prescription for depression. He also was referred for Alcoholics Anonymous group support meetings. So far Mike's treatment, (a combination of therapy, medication and the 12-step support group) is working, for he has not been back to the strip joints, bars or bottle. His normal personality is gradually returning. His spirituality continues to grow. Mike lost himself for awhile and he is slowly finding his way back.

Addictions Pulled by addictions into a dark tunnel A battle of Good vs. Evil to fight. It was grace and love that brought us through As together we journeyed into God's light.

...Karen Valiant

The Battle of Good vs. Evil

The following song captures the essence of a lost soul. It is from the album *The Big Picture,* by Elton John. The lyrics of this song have spoken to both my husband and myself as we began the battle of Good versus Evil. *Recover Your Soul* by Elton John, copyright 1997, William A. Borg Ltd.

>Baby you're missing
>Something in the air.
>I gotta name but it don't matter.
>What's going on? It's cold in here.
>You have a life but it's torn and tattered.
>Maybe you're losing Pieces of your heart.
>You have a world but it stopped turning.
>You lose the day And gain the dark.
>Love was a fire but it stopped burning.
>Chorus: So spare your heart; save your soul.
>Don't drag your love across the coals.
>Find your feet and your fortune can be told.
>Release, relax, let go.
>And hey now let's recover,
>And hey now let's recover,
>Hey now let's recover your soul.
>Baby you're missing
>Something in the air.
>I gotta name but it don't matter.
>What's going on?
>It's cold in here.
>You have a life but it's torn and tattered.
>Repeat Chorus
>So spare your heart save your soul.
>Don't drag your love across the coals.
>Find your feet and your fortune can be told.

Release, relax, let go.
And hey now let's recover,
Hey now let's recover,
Hey now let's recover your soul.
Hey now let's recover your soul.

This story would not be complete without mention of what I am convinced is the *bigger picture*. I absolutely believe that my husband and I were involved in a battle of the forces of Good vs. Evil. I heard my husband describe himself as "having an emptiness in his heart" and being "angry at God" (feelings related to his brother's suicide). I have seen the evil piercing looks from my husband, so intense that I got goose bumps from fear. We were a perfect target, if evil agents exist. If our marriage could be destroyed by evil forces, then Evil has won once again.

When I first discovered the charge card statement, listing the nude dance clubs, I believe that something led me to look into the "secret porno" file. I could have easily found Mike's social security number in several other places. I believe something spiritual happened, directing me to be confronted with the pornography, just as something guided me to discover Mike's hidden cigarettes. Perhaps I had experienced the guidance of a "spiritual guardian angel." I have continued to feel a gentle guidance throughout this process, leading me to the helpful people, resources and even reaching me through the words of our pastor.

Mike and I were also blessed with the gift of the addictions counselor who was assigned to us by a public agency, a man who also happened to be a Christian. He especially helped Mike in emotional, psychological, and spiritual healing. I believe this male counselor was the perfect match for the situation and did not happen by coincidence.

Here is another example of the spiritual guidance working in my life. Just a few days after I learned of Mike's secret life, I had made a new friend, Geni. She must have sensed that something was wrong for she invited me to her home that same afternoon and insisted I visit. A complete stranger, only hours before, she took me into her home and her heart. I couldn't believe I was telling her the things that poured out of my mouth, but I did. Geni listened and supported me with unconditional love. She was kind enough to offer her home as shelter any time that I might need it. I never felt I needed shelter, but it was such a relief to know that I had found a safe haven. She and I still remain good friends today. She is my human guardian angel.

About six months after "all Hell broke loose," I also had the joy of experiencing the most brilliant rainbow that I have ever seen. It lasted only thirty seconds, while I was tearfully driving home from work and was feeling the hopelessness again. I believe the rainbow was a source of communication from above. It was my personal sign of hope. I felt exhilarated. If this is a battle of Good versus Evil, the evil force may have worked its way into our lives, but Good had prevailed.

Perhaps the most dramatic example of the spiritual realm happened one night in January. While we were sleeping, I awoke to the eerie feeling that someone was watching me. I looked toward my husband and I could see him asleep, with his head on the pillow. But I could also see a frightening spiritlike image of him sitting up and lustfully looking at me. It appeared to look like Mike, but it was an evil, dirty image of him. I bolted up in our bed and yelled "Get out of here!" That spirit literally jumped out of his body and flew out of our bedroom. I woke poor Mike up, with all the commotion. Perhaps I dreamed the whole event. Who knows? But after that night, Mike expressed how much better he felt. He *is* better and we are still together. We take one day at a time, and are looking forward to our 15th anniversary of our old marriage, the 1st year of our new life.

Dealings

So that is our story. My hope is that, by sharing our experiences, I will be able to help others understand the complex journey that one goes through as the spouse of a sex addict. Perhaps other spouses will realize that they are not alone.

I do not, however, want to leave anyone feeling hopeless, so the rest of this book has been written to help a person deal with all of this. It does seem overwhelming at first but let me share a few guidelines.

1. Do maintain your highest level of integrity, even when you feellike striking back.
2. Take extra special care of yourself. This includes monitoringyour own eating, sleeping, exercising and relaxation activities. Are they healthy?
3. Seek professional help for yourself.
4. Seek out a support group.
5. Journal your feelings and his activities.
6. At first, carefully document work schedules, expenses and phone calls. As the trust gradually rebuilds your vigilance can lessen.
7. Take over all finances, at least temporarily. Also seek professional financial guidance if needed. There may me exorbitant outstanding bills.
8. Have your spouse/significant other request copies of all chargecard and bank account transactions for the time period in question. He/she may need to request that for you, in writing.
9. Take the charge cards and ATM bank cards into your possession, at least temporarily.
10. Open all mail.
11. Ask questions about the work schedule (especially excessivehours) and unusual phone calls.
12. Get involved with a group that will support you spiritually.
13. See a doctor to be tested for STD's. Also seek medical attention for any related stress-induced illnesses or conditions.

14. Set your limits and guidelines for recovery.
15. Encourage your spouse/significant other to seek professional help.
16. Insist that your spouse/significant other take a lie detector test, if he does not confess to sexual intercourse. If he refuses, assume he has had sexual intercourse.
17. Encourage your spouse/significant other to get involved with a 12-step program.
18. You get involved in a 12-step program, such as ALANON or
19. COSA.
20. Together get involved in a support group such as Recovering Couples Anonymous (RCA)[11].
21. Use the internet or library or purchase books, and continue to educate yourself about addictions.
22. Keep talking, talking, talking.
23. Pray.
24. Never ever blame yourself for what has happened.
25. Trust that your true friends will support you. You can talk with them about it.
26. Set clear boundaries for acceptable/unacceptable behaviors in your relationship.
27. Take one day at a time. If you believe that your spouse/significant other is sincerely working toward recovery, stick with it, but if he/she is not, LEAVE THAT RELATIONSHIP AND BELIEVE THAT YOU ARE WORTHY OF BETTER.

Organized Immorality

It is time for all of us to wake up to the concept of organized immorality. Pornography* is rampant in our society. We find it in books, magazines, mailings, movies, and now, the powerful internet. We and our children are being exploited. As quickly as a well-meaning family learns to block or filter out certain television programming or internet sites, someone in this world finds a way to slip more pornography through. Seemingly innocent websites are used to trick us into stumbling onto pornographic sites. According to a 1997 report put out by the National Coalition for the Protection of Children and Families(NCPCF)*, the Playboy website alone had received 4.7 million hits in one seven-day period. Pornography is easily accessible to an inquisitive child and there currently are no laws to prevent it. Pedophiles have easy access to our children through chat rooms. The NCPCF considers pornography a public health and safety issue.

If a person, out of curiosity, makes an internet inquiry to view X-rated pornography, that e-mail address enters a pool of slimy underworld business people. Your e-mail address suddenly begins receiving their pornographic offers. Cybersex is a term describing chat rooms or instant message boards on the worldwide web that allows explicit sexual conversations. It is available to anyone who owns a personal computer that is serviced by an internet system.

Take a look at the local want ads. You will see a newspaper making money off of classifieds looking to hire 18-year-old nude dancers. Or glance at the many ads of call girls soliciting business. Check out the entertainment and/or sports sections and you'll find some interesting ads enticing people to nude dance clubs.

Once a person uses a charge card at one of the strip joints or nude dance clubs, it won't be long before he/she will begin receiving odd phone calls, such as supposed "singles clubs" wanting to speak with him/her. Or there is the woman who doesn't identify herself but asks for your significant other, by name. She swiftly hangs up when you identify yourself. Try the "*69" keys on your phone, to get the number of the last person who called and guess what? In almost all cases, it will be a "blocked number." Once I managed to talk with one of the solicitors and asked how she got my husband's name. She said it was on "a list." I told her he was married and to take it off the list.

We have since received no more of those kind of phone calls.

You hear about stag parties. The strippers are more than half-dressed sexy dancers. Private parties allow much more than the "look don't touch" rule that has been fed to us for so long. Here is a letter written in our local newspaper just a week ago (May 25, 1999):

Written To: Carolyn Hax, of the Washington Post Writers Group, for the "Tell Me About It" Column

Dear Carolyn: My boyfriend will be attending a string of bachelor parties for his friends in the next couple of months, and I'm sure some will be pretty raunchy, with strip bars or strippers on the agenda. Besides the fact that I don't want him hanging around naked women, I think participation in this kind of thing is degrading to humans in the extreme. He dislikes the idea of strip bars, but he wants to be with his friends, so he is going to go. The feminist voice in me says, "No way, it's wrong. I'm not going to compromise my beliefs"—yet I'm in love, so what's a girl to do?

How and why do women put up with men engaging in crude behavior? I'm sure there are other feminists in love out there who are dealing with similar issues.

—E.H.

Basically the response of the writer endorsed the participation in the stag parties, as long as the "beau can look, but not touch" and "didn't enjoy it". So the media message went out to millions of readers that these behaviors were okay.

The John Gray (famous author of the Mars/Venus books) column from the Los Angeles Times, which was printed in a local newspaper one week later (June 1), seems to handle the problem more realistically:

Don't let boyfriend's indiscretion derail relationship

Dear John: I found out that Brad, my boyfriend of three years, went to my cousin's bachelor party and got out of control with one of the strippers. Some of these girls were also hookers.

Brad was completely sober, so alcohol was not an excuse. He didn't have sex with any of them, but I found out in detail what occurred that night. I was shocked and feel that he went too far.

I initially broke up with him. He finally called me a couple of days later.

I had calmed down and we talked. I decided to forgive him, but I just couldn't forget. A month later, we broke up because I couldn't deal with the fact that he had been intimate with someone else.

I know his actions were purely out of lust, but I can't stop thinking about it. Brad very much regrets what he did. With every conversation we have now, we both end up crying. He can't live with himself for what he has done. He has always been faithful to me except for this one time. Should we completely cut off all contact with each other? Is there a right or wrong way to deal with this? Why do guys feel like it is OK to act in a way that would be totally unacceptable in another environment? Please tell me how we both can go forward from here.

—Shocked in Pomona, California The response:

Dear Shocked: "On that night, your boyfriend got out of control: An opportunity that looked like fun presented itself, and he took it. Was this right? Of course not. Did he act in an immature and improper manner? You bet he did.

Does he regret what he has done? Most definitely. Will he do it again? Not if he's smart and wants to hold onto you. Everyone makes mistakes and deserves a second chance. Hopefully, he has learned from his mistake. Take some time to let your emotions cool off. Then let your heart and your head weigh the options. If you do indeed love him, allow him back into your life with the understanding that another indiscretion will be the end of the beautiful thing you have together. If he cares, he will never hurt you again. Good luck with getting your lives back on track."

I am not saying that these last two examples of human behavior represent sexual addiction. However, the curiosity raised at the stag parties may entice men to become more involved with the perverse pleasure they experienced. Any person can make a mistake, but repeating the mistake over and over again represents addiction. This experience may simply wet the appetite for more perverse pleasures. Other experiences might include sex clubs. Some sex clubs allow people to literally watch others having sex, not on a videotape but in person. Cabarets or strip joints don't only have one room for the general paying public, but they also have private rooms, for a nude dancer to dance only for your husband/boyfriend and then to sit, naked, by him or on him, to "talk" about his and/or her problems. Basically the girls are taught to form a "relationship" with your man. It doesn't stop at the club. She then solicits his return visits with titillating phone calls to his home and his workplace. It is all a big, organized business to get more of his (and your) money.

Don't be surprised if you also start receiving unusual mail…gifts? We received a collection of odd things, from mail order ads, to the Sports Illustrated Swimsuit gift collection. Question all mail and all strange phone calls.

So Now the Paranoia is Setting In

Expect to become somewhat paranoid. Since your world as you knew it has suddenly been turned upside down, it stands to reason that you don't know what is real and what is make-believe. You will begin to question everything, to the extreme. You will be extra sensitive to newscasts about sex clubs, newspaper stories about sex clubs, television themes on shows about sex clubs, sexual addiction in politics, strippers in movies, and sexually explicit jokes. It will seem as if perverted sex is the daily topic being discussed everywhere.

Ask lots of questions about any minute questionable behavior. You may even embarrass yourself a few times by being way "off base" several times, but this watchfulness is healthy and a good tool to use in the long-term recovery process. A man who is truly invested in his recovery will be tolerant as you experience your paranoia. As we worked with our counselor, he once asked me, "What % of trust will tell you that you two are okay?" We agreed that I was aiming for 90% trust but that it is healthy and realistic to reserve that other 10% of doubt so that I never get too complacent.

Triggers

As in any crisis, there will be triggers. These are smaller events which will remind us of the critical incident. A trigger might be a billboard or newspaper ad for nude dance clubs, or a song's lyrics that express your pain or loss. It might be an article of clothing that your husband wore when with another woman or a talk show topic, a joke, a T.V. show or a movie clip. It could be anything, anytime and it is usually unexpected.

If you liken the main event (discovery of the betrayal) to the initial shock of an earthquake, the triggers are the future "aftershocks." They continue to come in waves but in lesser and lesser measurable amounts. Eventually you will again reach a peaceful level but it may take months or even years. You may think you have achieved that peaceful level and then a trigger will throw you right back into the emotional abyss. Hopefully you will learn ways to pull yourself up out of that abyss, more easily each time. Be very, very patient with yourself when dealing with these inevitable triggers.

Perhaps the most challenging part of my emotional recovery was learning how to erase the persistent visual images each time they popped into my head. I have devised a step-by-step image destruction plan that seems to work. The imagery goes something like this: It is Mike's last visit to the "gentlemen's club." My husband is sitting at a table in a private room, watching his favorite nude dancer perform for him. She, at first, appears beautiful, seductive and muscular. As she bends down close to Mike's face, to begin sucking out his soul, he catches a glimpse of two small Satanic horns poking out from her head. He is startled. His trance is broken. He becomes aware of the evil around him and pushes himself away from the table. Her appearance quickly changes: she has weeping sores all over her body (apparently from some sort of disease), her hair is filled with head lice (apparently from some other patrons) and her skin begins to sag and wrinkle right before his eyes. Mike's fantasy sex goddess suddenly sickens him. He jumps up to leave. She tries to go after him but as she gets off the table in haste, she accidentally steps onto a land mine and explodes into a million harmless pieces. She is gone. Mike is free of her. Our journey through recovery begins.

I know the imagery seems violent and childlike, but it worked for me. At one point my imagination made the dancer look so disgusting that even I didn't want to go there (to the image) anymore. Use your own imagination to do whatever is necessary (in your mind) to clear out the negative "stuff."

If you ever happen to be driving around and you see a billboard advertising a cabaret or "gentlemen's club", try to feel sorry for anyone who would find themselves in those "gentlemen's clubs." Where did that name ever originate, anyway? "Gentleman" just doesn't seem to fit the situation! How about, "Voyeurist's club" or "Pervert's club?"

These examples may help you see that you have the power to reduce the impact of the future triggers in your life. Use imagery, empathy and humor to help you win this battle.

Who Is to Blame Anyway?

One of the most frustrating consequences of a man's sexual misbehavior is that the whole world seems determined to pin the blame onto someone, and it usually blames the woman. What need was she not fulfilling? Why didn't he go to her for comfort instead of someone else? Was she pressuring him too much? Was she too controlling? Was she too frigid? Did she make him feel less of a man? Did she make him feel powerless, unimportant or inferior? Just what was he missing, that he had to go out and get "it" somewhere else?

It is important that you not get caught up in the blame game. It will distract you from recovery. Remember that even the most loving, wellmeaning, warm, beautiful person can be in relationship with an addictive personality. It is also extremely important to understand that the person with the addiction is not in any way doing those behaviors to hurt their committed partner. If you find yourself unable to let go of the self-blame or self-shame, it is important for you to seek professional help. Oftentimes there are other related underlying issues or belief systems which may go very deep and/or very much in the past, that you will need to therapeutically challenge. Before one can completely heal, he/she must lay the blame and shame to rest.

The Reaction of His Family

At some point, your situation will reach the level of your husband's family. Do not expect them to believe you or support you. If his family is supportive consider yourself fortunate. Chances are that the addictive personality has been raised in a dysfunctional[14] home. His family may deny any problem and may bond together to support him and him alone. You may appear to be a paranoid, sick, trouble-maker who has somehow caused the "problem," if they can even recognize that there really is a problem. They may be completely entrenched in denial.

Some of his family members may stop talking with you completely, out of loyalty toward him. Others will dismiss everything and pretend it didn't happen. Others might actively work toward dismantling your marriage or relationship. Still others may actively seek you out to talk it out.

Educate yourself about sexual addiction, alcohol addiction and dysfunctional family systems. It will help you understand that you are not crazy and you are not to blame. One of the best resources for understanding dysfunctional families is a book entitled, Adult Children, The Secrets of Dysfunctional Families, authored by John Friel and Linda Friel. Mike's aunt sent me a copy, believing it might help me better understand the workings of his biological family.

The crisis may encourage dialogue between you and his family members that have been "pushed away" from the immediate dysfunctional family unit. If an aunt or uncle or sibling confides in you, gather up as much information as possible regarding your spouse's/boyfriend's family system. It can help you and him better understand the family dynamics. Sex addicts oftentimes have a history of child neglect, abuse or sexually perverted values in their background. What were the values and morals used to raise his family? Try to piece together any family history of alcoholism, manic/depression, sex addiction, or divorce. This information will help you both as you work with the professionals.

Your Own Friends and Family

Speaking with your own friends and family is perhaps the hardest challenge. Because of the embarrassment, humiliation and shame that accompanies sexual addiction, it is extremely difficult to talk with your own family and friends. Our society is still not comfortable talking about sexual addiction. In general there is a misunderstanding of exactly what it is. Unfortunately most persons equate sexual addiction with child molestation and they do not have enough information to know that there are many levels/types of sexual addiction. When our society is uncomfortable about a situation or issue it commonly reacts with fear, anger and rage, or blame. Speaking with friends and family carries a certain risk.

It has been almost a year since I first discovered our situation and I still have only confided (the unedited version) with three people: my sister (the counselor) and my two closest friends. I called my best friend first but this I did several days after I discovered the "problem" and only after I had built enough courage to share the situation. My husband wanted me to keep it all a secret, of course, but that is simply impossible. That is not fair to you. Do **not** keep this to yourself. The burden is too big to carry around on your own.

My sister, who normally is very open-minded and tolerant, used words like "hate" and "kill." She strongly urged me to run for safety's sake. In a later conversation, after she had a chance to calm down, she shared with me the fact that the Chinese culture has two symbols for "crisis;" one stands for danger and the other for opportunity. What wonderful wisdom! This was in fact a very dangerous time in our marriage, but it could turn out to be an opportunity for growth and understanding.

A month after I discovered the crisis in our lives, my closest friend spent three days with me, miles away from our home. By coincidence, we had already planned her visit weeks before. What was first meant to be a fun reunion with my best buddy became a tension-filled, emotional event. Her mission was simply to talk me into leaving Mike. She was so angry with him that she couldn't allow herself to be in the same room with him.

Karen Valiant

The only way she would come here is if I promised to pick her up at the airport and immediately drive far away from Mike. She and her husband were our two dearest friends who loved us both. They too were feeling extremely responsible and betrayed. Even knowing Mike as well as they did, one of their greatest concerns was whether or not he also had child pornography in his secret collection. Friends and family members share in the shock and confusion.

    I still have not told the whole story to the rest of my family. Nor have I explained my extreme grief and troubled situation to my peers at work. Until more people become enlightened about sexual addiction, it may bring more harm than good, I reasoned, so I kept my mouth shut.

    Remember that the people who truly love you will come through for you. That brings me to my own children. What do you say to the children? Consider their maturity, their circumstance and their relationship with your husband/significant other. My children are 18 and 21 years old. My daughter was home (another coincidence?) when I discovered Mike's visits to the underworld abyss, so she dealt with my reactions firsthand. She was a lifesaving support for me. Children will naturally be very angry, blunt and painfully insightful but they may also be your greatest advocates. Initially all three of our children advised me to run away from Mike, as fast as I could. Don't worry about the new house; just get out of there! I believe my actions modeled behavior that I hope will help them all if they should ever encounter crises with their loved ones. They witnessed my grief, my confusion and my example of love and its unbelievable ability to overcome tremendous odds. They learned about the healing power of forgiveness. They have all assured me that they will follow my lead; should I choose to stay in this marriage they will accept that decision and if we should choose to go our separate ways they will understand. They still witness a persistence in our commitment that they do not fully understand yet they are learning to respect.

Forgiveness

When does forgiveness happen? It is difficult to put a timeframe on it, because each situation is so unique and each person journeys through this at their own pace. Some personalities never allow themselves to feel forgiveness toward another human being who has wronged them.

There are many good books about forgiveness and many touching accounts about grace. Our pastor defined grace as "the ability to give the gift of forgiveness to someone who doesn't deserve it." I remember the short period of separation that we went through; necessary for me because I was far too alienated, angry and steeped in grief to even want to be physically near Mike. I needed the distance to help me think more clearly, to sort through the myriad of emotions, thoughts and decisions which were assaulting me. Eventually we shared the same home again but I had a very difficult time sharing intimacy. Our physical relationship was distorted. We were both so reserved with one another. We were extremely sensitive toward one another and very careful of everything we said and did. It was like walking on eggshells. In hindsight I would recommend a lengthier separation, to avoid the discomforts and confusion. However, by being together, we were both forced to trudge through the "stuff." While in the midst of this experience it seemed that only a miracle could bring about forgiveness.

Finally one day, about a month into the journey, I blurted out to Mike that I forgave him. This was said after yet another strained discussion about us divorcing and trying to decide if it would just be better for both of us, to part our ways. Neither of us wanted to hurt the other or experience the other's pain. That "declaration of forgiveness" was only the first step in forgiving him. Mike wrote the following letter in response to my declaration: 10/20/98

My Dearest Karen,
I am so very sorry for the pain and suffering that I have caused you. I will do everything in my power to make it up to you and gain back your trust. I know in my heart that if I don't drink again, the events of these past few months will never happen again. The real Mike would never do

those things and you must believe that. You also must believe that you were not the cause of my behavior and it was not done to intentionally hurt you. Above *all*, you must believe that I did not have sex with anyone and that was never even in my mind. I was caught up in the ego boosting the attention gave me and I was very weak for some time. I am not proud of my weakness and again, I am so so very sorry.

The thought of living without you is the hardest thing to deal with. We may have our problems at times as all couples do, but I know our love and caring for each other can get us through the bad times.

Thank-you most of all for saying you forgive me. That means so much to me.

All my love,
Mike

In reality, it took many more months before I can say I truly did forgive him completely. Our counselor helped me see that Mike was ill when he was on his mission of self-destruction. Sometimes I believed that "forgive and forget" was the only way to go and then two days later, the anger and rage would show cause to forget about forgiveness and instead forget the entire marriage. A sermon helped me hear the message that forgiveness was necessary while we are not expected to forget. Do not expect to ever completely forget what has happened. It is healthy to gradually dwell on it less and less but it is also healthy for both of you to remember what happened, how it happened, and why it happened. It is imperative that the man physically, psychologically and emotionally walks through the pain with you and that, through continued AA meetings and/or other 12-step support groups, he is reminded of the wreck that his addictions caused.

Before you can forgive him, you first need to completely forgive yourself. Forgive yourself for falling in love with a guy who would hurt you so deeply. Forgive yourself for working so hard saving and sacrificing money, only to have him so quickly "blow it" on his own selfish, destructive pleasures. Forgive yourself for exposing your children to such immorality and loss of innocence. You tried to raise them in a healthy way. Now the joke is on you, that you had no control over the immoral behaviors of your own husband. Forgive yourself for allowing yourself to live the lie with your husband. Forgive yourself in case there was something that you may have inadvertently done to cause this. Forgive yourself for naively trusting the man you married. He has made quite the fool out of you. Will you ever trust your intuition again?

Victimization

I had been the victim of sexual addiction. Now I must make many difficult decisions. Should we separate or not? For how long? Should we divorce? Are we both committed to positive changes in our relationship? Is he willing to change? Am I? Are we right for each other?

The important lesson here is to *take action* or forever remain "the victim." A person can wallow for just so long in the pain and suffering that sexual addiction brings. At some point, I must choose to divorce the old marriage (if not physically, at least do so symbolically). We must change the old dance steps and substitute them with new ones that are healthier. I absolutely must protect myself by taking action to insure my financial security. I will do whatever it takes to move myself out of the victim role. It can and will stifle growth, for it is so easy to get stuck in that rut.

Overcoming the Pain

Time is the great healer. Even after the three days of intense efforts by my sweet friend, to convince me to leave Mike, and even after I reached a point of knowing that I am fully capable of making things work in this life *on my own*, I still came to this conclusion: **I owe it to our marriage to give him a chance to recover.** If he will continue to work on positive changes, both he and our marriage will be better. It's a win/win situation. In my heart I realize that if this marriage doesn't survive, I have no desire to seek life with another man, so what is there to lose? I'll either remain married and hopefully happier or divorced and bitterly alone. I can honestly say there are no regrets. However, if I had never given Mike the opportunity to work on his recovery, I know I would have regretted it. Will your actions leave no regrets?

I also believe that our life events happen for a reason. I can now honestly say I am thankful that Mike's manic/depression and alcohol addiction and the resulting sexual addiction were all brought to light. Had I not discovered the evidence that uncovered Mike's secret life, he would still be drinking today and who knows where that would have led him? Had he not been diagnosed by the psychiatrist, would he have ever gotten the medication he needed? If this was a test of our faith or our commitment to one another, I am up to the challenge. We all have choices. This was mine: see this through. The pain is still there, but it continues to lessen in time. The triggers are less frequent and not as intense. The fulfilling power of love has overcome the empty power of evil. I have been on a peace-seeking mission. At times I feel ambivalence about marriage. For the most part, I am at peace with myself. Mike is at peace with himself. We are seeking peace with each other.

Mike and I danced to the following song, performed by Michael Bolton. It captures the essence of our journey.

That's What Love is All About lyrics by Michael Bolton and E. Kaz, copyright 1987, CBS Inc., Columbia Records

Love Over Lust: How Love Overcame the Power of Addiction

There was a time
We thought our dream was over,
When you and I had surely reached the end.
Still here we are.
The flame as strong as ever,
All because we both kept holding on.
We know we can weather any storm.
Baby, that's what love is all about,
Two hearts that find a way, somehow,
To keep the fire burning.
It's something we could never live without.
If it takes forever,
We can work it out,
Beyond a shadow of a doubt.
Baby, that's what love is all about.
As time goes by, we've learned to rediscover
The reason why
This dream of ours survives.
Through thick and thin,
We're destined for each other.
Knowing we can reach the other side,
Far beyond the mountains of our pride.

CHORUS:
Ridin' the good times is easy.
The hard times can tear you apart.
There'll be times in your heart
When the feelin' is gone.
But ya keep on believing And ya keep holdin' on.
Baby, that's what love is all about,
Two hearts that find a way, somehow,
To keep the dream from dying.
It's something we could never live without.
If it takes forever, We can work it out,
Beyond a shadow of a doubt.
Baby, that's what love is all about.

Recovery of the Couple

A recovering couple is on the most important journey of their married life. Both partners must be involved in the healing process. They must be willing to work on their communication skills, development of intimacy and development of trust. They need time (at least a year) to continue actively working together on their recovery. They also each need the opportunity to work on their individual recovery issues, especially if those issues inhibit the couple's recovery process.

The first step in a couple's recovery is to admit that the old relationship is dead. Be relieved it is dead, for obviously it was not an entirely healthy one.

The second step in recovery is for each of you to make an assessment of where you are in your relationship and where you hope to be in the future. See if there is a commitment from both parties. Make a list of pros and cons regarding your relationship. Examine your common values, goals and dreams.

Relationship Inventory
Which of the negative behaviors/attitudes/belief can be changed? Which cannot?
What is/are the common cause(s) for the items that are negative?
Are there destructive patterns? If so, what are they?
Is there something therapeutically that can be done to prevent the negative behaviors/attitudes/beliefs from reoccurring? If so, what is the strategy? What do you need from each other? How can you better communicate these needs? What are your common dreams/goals? How do you envision your new relationship? How can you love each other without reservation?

The third step in recovery is to begin building an extremely strong foundation of trust. Absolute trust. Absolutely no dishonesty can be allowed for this to work. Even the smallest details must be honestly communicated, **no exceptions.** The man who has been involved in sexual addiction is a master of illusion. He can appear normal to others. He can be involved in worthwhile community activities. He can be a model employee at his workplace. However both of you now must be assured and re-assured that what you see is what is real. A person's true character is the one that happens in the partner's absence. Is your partner involved in honorable behaviors even when you are not around? Trust takes many, many months and opportunities for testing it, in order for it to begin growing again. The marriage partner who has been victimized needs proof that the other partner is worthy of trust. If trust is not there or not growing, it is time to re-examine your relationship.

The fourth step is to continue doing the first three steps over and over again. If at any time in the future, your spouse breaks the trust, then it is up to you to decide whether you want to begin this cycle again or whether it is time for you to jump off the treadmill.

It is important that both partners seek professional and group support during the first year of sexual addiction recovery. Oftentimes the couple is facing the complications of multiple addictions and co-dependency and/or family dysfunction. The journey is complex and long but it can be powerfully enriching.

> Face the worst
> Think the best
> Do your most and
> Leave the rest .
>
> Author Unknown

Nine Months Later

Mike and I are still together. Life is not all rosy but we have made a lot of progress. We are taking one day at a time. Mike is still not drinking, not smoking and not involved in his sexual addiction. I have accepted that Mike has an addictive personality and he especially acts out when under stress. He was sick.

Mike's amount of stress has lessened as we settled into our new home and neighborhood. His father passed away after a long illness so the additional pressures related to his illness have lessened. Mike changed jobs so that we now have more time off together.

We have made some positive changes. We both continue to grow in our understanding of addictions by reading, gathering internet information and participating in group support. Mike continues with his medication for depression and meets with a psychiatrist every three months. He practices daily reading, meditation and prayer. We continue to grow spiritually through church participation, prayer and readings.

Mike is now better able to reflect upon our crisis in search of the answers to "How" and "Why" but it is still difficult for him to talk about it. He is just now beginning to consider himself as a sex addict, for he equated sex addict with sex offender and knew he wasn't that extreme. He is at least now ready to learn about sexual addiction although he would prefer to leave all of this in the past. We are both committed to our future together, perhaps even more bonded because of our past trauma. A more mature love has been born from this human tragedy.

We are learning about intimacy, tolerance, intolerance, verbal and nonverbal expression, humility, understanding and empathy. We are more attuned to the human spirit; its courage and its frailties.

We realize that this journey is not over. It involves a tremendous amount of hard work and dedication. We both feel, at this point, that our marriage is worth the effort. I am ready to stop shedding tears of sadness because of our crisis. I am now prepared to bury all the pain and suffering permanently; lay it to rest so that I can continue moving forward.

I have recently managed to be apart from my husband, first for five days and now, for two weeks, and I can honestly say that I am learning to let go.

Mike clearly knows the consequences if he chooses to go down the addictions pathway again. I know that I needed the rest periods, to nurture myself. I needed the "aloneness" brought by our time apart, to really practice the process of letting go. He needs time apart from me, also, to learn that he is very capable of being alone and making good choices.

I believe Mike and I have "faced the worst." I still need to work on the concept of "think the best." For many years I did so and, in this situation, I got very hurt. So for the past nine months, I have swung to the opposite extreme; I have been expecting the worst. Now it is time to try to get back to thinking the best of each other. It is also time to "leave the rest". It is time to let go and let God take it from here. Mike's actions and hard work have helped me see that I can gradually let go of that negative outlook and return to the trusting person I normally am. It is easy for him to know that he is doing honorable things but it seems like it has taken me forever to believe it even again possible. So I continue to work on my attitude adjustment.

We are both "doing our most" as we continue to work on our relationship issues. However I still find myself with an enormous amount of passionate energy when I re-visit the topic of sexual addiction. It helps me to direct that energy toward productive activities such as letters to the editor, phone calls to the village board, phone calls to the newspaper's reader advocate, organizing a citizen's group to work toward cleaning up our local newspaper and community's advertising, and, of course, writing this book. You could join or support any number of local and/or national organizations that are fighting pornography, cybersex or sex clubs. You could find your own unique avenue for action. And then remember to "leave the rest".

"Can the Ethiopian change his skin or the leopard change his spots? Then also you can do good who are accustomed to do evil. I will scatter you like chaff driven by the wind from the desert. This is your lot, the portion I have measured out to you, says the Lord, because you have forgotten me and trusted in lies.

I myself will lift up your skirts over your face, and your shame will be seen.

Karen Valiant

    I have seen your abominations, your adulteries and neighing, your lewd harlotries, on the hills in the field.
    Woe to you, O Jerusalem!
    How long will it be before you are made clean?"
    Jeremiah 13: 23-27 The Holy Bible Revised Standard Version

The Future

Just as a leopard cannot change its spots, an addict cannot change his/her genetic predisposition toward addiction. For the purpose of clarity, I am defining an addiction as any behavior which has an outcome that is unpredictable and that behavior is repeated, in spite of negative consequences. He or she was born with tendencies toward addiction and will always be that way. Remember that once an addict, always an addict. The biological makeup of that person is something over which he/she has no control. Fortunately, in this time of medical miracles, however, there may be help for an addictive personality. By seeing a psychiatrist or medical doctor, one can be prescribed helpful medicine, to regulate the brain chemicals involved in the pleasure-seeking area. There may also be underlying depression that needs medical and/or therapeutic attention. Or perhaps a fullblown manic-depressive episode needs treatment. Counseling can help build the necessary skills for a more open communication of needs and feelings. Eventually the addict learns to replace the sick fantasy world with healthy pleasures based in reality.

So is there a bright future for an addict? Absolutely, as long as he/she defines exactly what the addiction is and faces the addiction boldly and honestly, he/she can take action to prevent himself/herself from being controlled by that addiction.

The point is that if you know you are an addict in any area, unless you want to become a prisoner to that addiction, you have to take steps to avoid any involvement with that addictive situation or substance. You need to rebuild your spirituality, to give you the strength and direction necessary to win the battle. You need to develop a life-long coping strategy while celebrating each individual day's successful sobriety. The rest of your future depends on it. The rest of your future is up to you and you alone.

Are you ready to make yourself clean and sober?

If you are in a relationship with an addict and you wish to remain in that relationship, you too can have a bright future. As long as the addict avoids his/her addictions and is working on his/her sobriety, it is only fair that you give the relationship a chance. It will be up to you to clearly set your limits. Carefully but lovingly let the addict know exactly what you are willing to tolerate and what the real consequences will be, should they fail to avoid the addiction. Your goal is to move toward complete forgiveness and understanding while enforcing honest, realistic boundaries. Remember that life still offers no guarantee that your partner will remain clean and sober. Most importantly, don't give up too soon. Give love enough time to work its miracle in overcoming the power of addictions, including lust.

If your partner fails, you must be firm, following through with the consequences, just as you said you would, **no matter how much it hurts at the time.** It *is* all about love. One must sometimes love his/herself enough to emotionally detach from a destructive partner. You truly are better off without the addicted person if they choose to remain in their addiction prison. Sometimes an addict must lose absolutely everything of importance before he/she bottoms out and seeks recovery. You do not have to be imprisoned along with them. Remember that you always have the key to get out!

Postscript

An important part of each person's life is the legacy one leaves for future generations. *Love Over Lust* is my attempt to emphasize the sinister impact that lust can have in our lives and the hope for healing that love offers. I want my children to understand that, when we make a lifetime commitment, that commitment will sometimes be challenged. It is then our responsibility to carefully evaluate the relationship. If both partners are working on recovery, that relationship is worth the effort. Yet one must love himself/herself enough to make difficult, healthy decisions, even if it means separating from an uncooperative mate. Healing can become a spiritual journey in the lives of both partners.

While traveling the long drive home from Los Angeles to Phoenix this past spring, my daughter and I had many hours to talk and listen to music. We were reflecting upon the events of the past two years. She was there for me the day I discovered the betrayal. Since then, she has witnessed my slow healing process. She had re-read my final manuscript and, in her frank, comical way, informed me that she simply could not allow me to end the book the way I did. Instead she shared her sensitivity to our spiritual journey and she clearly understood our renewed commitment to our marriage vows. She dedicated the following song to me, her step-dad and *Love Over Lust*. May it inspire us all to never lose faith in the miraculous healing power of love.

> That's The Way It Is
> Written by M. Martin, K. Lundin, A. Carlson Sung by Celine Dion
> From Celine; All the Way, A Decade of Song, 1999
>
> I can read your mind,
> And I know your story.
> I see what you're going through, yeah.
> It's an uphill climb and I'm feeling sorry,
> But I know it will come to you, girl.

Karen Valiant

Don't surrender 'cause you can win,
In this thing, girl.
Chorus:
When you want it the most
There's no easy way out.
When you're ready to go
And your heart's left in doubt.
Don't give up on your faith.
Love comes to us who believe it.
And that's the way it is.

When you ask me for a simple answer,
I don't know what to say, no.
But it's plain to see if you stick together,
You're gonna find a way, yeah.
So don't surrender 'cause you can win.
In this thing, girl.

Chorus:
When you want it the most
There's no easy way out.
When you're ready to go
And your heart's left in doubt.
Don't give up on your faith.
Love comes to us who believe it.
And that's the way it is.

When life is empty with no tomorrow
And loneliness starts to call.
Baby, don't worry; forget your sorrow
'Cause love's going to conquer it all.

Chorus:
When you want it the most
There's no easy way out.
When you're ready to go
And your heart's left in doubt.
Don't give up on your faith

Love Over Lust: How Love Overcame the Power of Addiction

Love comes to us who believe it.
And that's the way it is.
Chorus:
That's the way it is.
That's the way it is, baby.
Don't give up on your faith.
Love comes to us who believe it.
And that's the way it is.

Epilogue:
20 Years Later

"In love the other is important; in lust you are important." - Osho

Over these past twenty years, since I first published this book, I have had plenty of time to ponder the meaning of lust and love. I have concluded that the sexual addiction, described in this book, was not the only problem. It was a by-product of a more comprehensive addiction. Mike would tell you that his choice to be in relationship with alcohol is what led to his chemically altered personality and eventually to his sexual addiction. The consequence of his choice to sexually lust after someone else, was a weakened love relationship with me.

Others who have chosen to remain in relationship with their chemical addiction may be demonstrating their lust through uncontrolled shopping, workaholic tendencies, pornography, gambling, hoarding behaviors, manic-depressive behaviors or a loss of their touch with reality; just to name some of the consequences.

Lust can take many different forms. It could be lust for dominance or power, lust for material goods or even lust for an exaggerated sense of self-worth. The common denominator of lust is that it is self-serving, as the Osho quote clearly communicates "In love the other is important; in lust you are important."

So how did love win, in our story? Our formula for success was a combination of commitment to change, medication and therapy for Mike, couples therapy for us, spiritual growth and a huge dose of patience as the broken trust in our relationship took years to repair.

Fast forward to now. I am happy to report that we are still together and Mike is chemical free. We are strapped and challenged by the restrictions of living in a COVID-19 existence. An assortment of masks fill the corner of our kitchen drawer. We dream of and prepare for vacations that we were forced to re-schedule, due to the travel risks. We pray for the successful development of a vaccine and a heightened sense of community, where the wearing or not wearing of masks is no longer considered a political statement.

We are literally squeezed into a two-bedroom apartment with our two pets as we build another new home, this time to downsize. Although this is a temporary situation, it definitely accentuates our current isolated existence.

It is Sunday. Our church is closed, as most still are, due to the airborne nature of the virulent, dangerous COVID-19 virus. We prepare to re-open the church doors, hopefully, by the end of this extremely long year but at least for the time being church will not be the same. There will be no group singing, no choral anthem, no hymnals, no hugs, no handshakes, no offering plate being passed, no communion plate and cup being passed and we will worship within a social distancing model. Live streaming has been the only way we have been able to experience a live sermon. ZOOM meetings have been somewhat helpful but we all long for fellowship with each other.

All of this heightened fear, increased anxiety, cancellation of events, depression, loss of relationship with our family, friends and neighbors have created a profound sense of grief. Some of us have lost loved ones; we have all been impacted by the loss of "normalcy" in our lives. We have lost our freedom to safely navigate our physical world. Theatres are still closed, in an apocalyptic way, as our local theatres eerily display March 2020 billboards announcing movies that are "coming soon" and yet most new releases never made it to the big screens. There is even talk that movie theatres may become a thing of the past. So much loss, sadness and fear...

Almost ten percent of our workforce is still unemployed while hundreds of thousands of Americans have already died during this pandemic. We await the day that we can receive a safe COVID-19 vaccine and/or we develop a herd immunity so that we can begin living a somewhat normal life again. Bottom line; we are going through tough times!

There has been a noted uptick in our society's use of alcohol and drugs (illegal and legal) as people seek ways to cope with our new COVID-19 existence. Yet we, Mike and I, are finding healthy ways to cope. This pandemic has had a way of accentuating both the good and the bad. More than ever, we have been compelled to find ways to safely entertain ourselves; spending more time with Nature, reading, learning new hobbies and re-visiting old ones. In this pandemic, all of us are forced to examine what is most important to us as we journey through it.

Mike and I are together and enjoying each other in our addiction-free lives. The main point here is that we are still in a positive, fulfilling relationship. I am not going to claim it has been easy. There are times that I continue to feel the tug of past hurts; with my own insecurities and memories; ones which could drag me back into that pit of distrust and despair. Mike, as he promised me twenty years ago, has done everything in his power to prove to me that he can be trusted. Even with all these latest stressors, Mike has "stayed the course" of his sobriety. There is absolutely no evidence of him falling back into his destructive relationships.

There is hope for all who struggle with addiction, to face that powerful force head-on and to rise above it. Although our story focused upon sexual addiction, that was how Mike's chemical addiction to alcohol affected our lives. His use of alcohol weakened his spirit and changed his personality. It took about six months, once Mike stopped drinking, for his real personality to gradually re-emerge. It has taken me years to learn to trust that the "real Mike" is here to stay but I know now that we have emerged through the other side of that dark tunnel of despair.

We are in a loving relationship. Life is good. We have survived Mike's cancer ten years ago, the death and loss of all our parents and several of our siblings and we are both now retired. We feel equipped to overcome whatever stresses life sends our way. Spiritually we are in a good place. Even though we do not have the freedom to physically enjoy the comradery and fellowship of our family, friends and community to the extent we desire, we begin each day with our morning inspirational readings and with meditation. We have learned to feed our souls, are extremely grateful and look forward to a bright future.

So I write this epilogue today, to give you hope that while life will continue to throw challenges your way, you can use those life experiences to complete a self-examination of what is truly important. You can use your wisdom to motivate yourself to generate a life plan or to create a positive life change. You have the strength to alter your immediate environment, if it needs some adjustment, to live a healthier and more satisfying life. You can focus upon the quality of love relationships. Most importantly, you can love your way through anything!

APPENDICES

APPENDIX 1
The Twelve Steps of Alcoholics Anonymous

1. We admitted we were powerless over alcohol—that our lives had become unmanageable.
2. Came to believe that a Power greater than ourselves could restore us to sanity.
3. Made a decision to turn our will and our lives over to the care of God *as we understood Him.*
4. Made a searching and fearless moral inventory of ourselves.
5. Admitted to God, to ourselves, and to another human being the exact nature of our wrongs.
6. Were entirely ready to have God remove all these defects of character.
7. Humbly asked Him to remove our shortcomings.
8. Made a list of all persons we had harmed, and became willing to make amends to them all.
9. Made direct amends to such people wherever possible, except when to do so would injure them or others.
10. Continued to take personal inventory and when we were wrong promptly admitted it.
11. Sought through prayer and meditation to improve our conscious contact with God *as we understood Him,* praying only for knowledge of His will for us and the power to carry that out.
12. Having had a spiritual awakening as the result of these steps, we tried to carry this message to alcoholics, and to practice these principles in all our affairs.

In the recovery process for sex addiction, the word "lust" is substituted for "alcohol" and the phrase "sexual addicts" is substituted for "alcoholics". All of these same twelve steps are used.

Anyone who participates in a 12-step program, learns to experience life one day at a time, as shared in the following poem. It is not the experience of today that drives us mad. It is the remorse or bitterness for something which happened yesterday.

Or the dread of what tomorrow may bring.

Let us therefore do our best to live but one day at a time.

...from Twenty-Four Hours a Day by Hazelden

THE SERENITY PRAYER

God grant me the serenity To accept the things I cannot change, The courage to change the things I can, And the wisdom to know the difference.

For your local Alcoholics Anonymous organization, look in the yellow pages, under Alcoholics Anonymous.

APPENDIX 2
AL-ANON

The Al-Anon Family groups are a fellowship of relatives and friends of alcoholics who share their experience, strength, and hope, in order to solve their common problems. We believe alcoholism is a family illness and that changed attitudes can aid recovery. Living with the effects of someone else's drinking is too devastating for most people to bear without help.

In Al-Anon we learn individuals are not responsible for another person's disease or recovery from it.

We let go of our obsession with another's behavior and begin to lead happier and more manageable lives, lives with dignity and rights; lives guided by a Power greater than ourselves.

In Al-Anon we learn:
- Not to suffer because of the actions or reactions of other people;
- Not to allow ourselves to be used or abused by others in theinterest of another's recovery;
- Not to do for others what they could do for themselves;
- Not to manipulate situations so others will eat, go to bed, get up,pay bills, not drink;
- Not to cover up for anyone's mistakes or misdeeds;
- Not to create a crisis;
- Not to prevent a crisis if it is in the natural course of events.

Detachment is neither kind nor unkind. It does not imply judgment or condemnation of the person or situation from which we are detaching. It is simply a means that allows us to separate ourselves from the adverse effects that another person's alcoholism can have upon our lives.

Detachment helps families look at their situations realistically and objectively, thereby making intelligent decisions possible.

Al-Anon is not allied with any sect, denomination, political entity, organization, or institution; does not engage in any controversy, neither endorses nor opposes any cause. There are no dues for membership. Al-Anon is self-supporting through its own voluntary contributions.

Al-Anon has but one purpose: to help families of alcoholics. We do this by practicing the Twelve Steps, by welcoming and giving comfort to families of alcoholics and by giving understanding and encouragement to the alcoholic.

Al-Anon Family Group Headquarters, Inc. **U.S. 1-800-356-9996**

APPENDIX 3

The Sexual Addiction Screening Test (SAST)
As Developed by Patrick Carnes, Ph.D. from *Contrary to Love*, 1989

The SAST provides a profile of responses which help to discriminate between addictive and nonaddictive behavior. To complete the test, answer each question by placing a check in the appropriate column.

YES NO
1. Were you sexually abused as a child or adolescent?
2. Have you subscribed or regularly purchased sexually explicit magazines like Playboy or Penthouse?
3. Did your parents have trouble with sexual behavior?
4. Do you often find yourself preoccupied with sexual thoughts?
5. Do you feel that your sexual behavior is not normal?
6. Does your spouse (or significant other(s)) ever worry or complain about your sexual behavior?

YES NO
7. Do you have trouble stopping your sexual behavior when you know it is inappropriate?
8. Do you ever feel bad about your sexual behavior?
9. Has your sexual behavior ever created problems for you or your family?
10. Have you ever sought help for sexual behavior you did not like?
11. Have you ever worried about people finding out about your sexual activities?
12. Has anyone been hurt emotionally because of your sexual behavior?
13. Are any of your sexual activities against the law?
14. Have you made promises to yourself to quit some aspect of your sexual behavior?

15. Have you made efforts to quit a type of sexual activity and failed?
16. Do you have to hide some of your sexual behavior from others?
17. Have you attempted to stop some parts of your sexual activity?
18. Have you ever felt degraded by your sexual behavior?
19. Has sex been a way for you to escape your problems?
20. When you have sex, do you feel depressed afterwards?
21. Have you felt the need to discontinue a certain form of sexual activity?
22. Has your sexual activity interfered with your family life?
23. Have you been sexual with minors?
24. Do you feel controlled by your sexual desire?
25. Do you ever think your sexual desire is stronger than you are?

The following significant observations were made by Dr. Carnes:
1. 96.5% of an addict sample population answered Yes to 13 or more questions.
2. The SAST results are appropriate for use in assessing men only.

APPENDIX 4

Partners of Sex Addicts

The following information is quoted and summarized from a pamphlet published by COSA, Co-dependents of Sexual Addiction. The group is an anonymous 12-step fellowship which is open to those whose lives have been affected by a person with sexually compulsive behaviors.

There are certain characteristics which describe a sexual co-dependent. They may include the following:

- lying, covering up, explaining away, or ignoring inappropriatesexual behaviors
- stifling the inner voice which tells us something is wrong
- accepting promises that "it won't happen again" many times over, and in effect, enabling the addiction
- increasing our efforts to control the addict
- telling ourselves that if only we could somehow change, for example, be more (or less) attractive, provocative, intelligent, competent, we could change another person's sexual behavior

Ultimately our efforts to control fail. The consequences leave us in despair: our self-esteem, personal boundaries and values are seriously compromised. Our health and our lives are at risk, and our identity is lost. We realize our need to reach out for help.

With support groups, we begin to experience relief from our isolation, in the safety of an anonymous gathering with others who share our stories. Little by little, sanity, clarity and our own truth begin to emerge. In our relationships, we learn detachment and become more fully present. In continued recovery, we live our lives in deeper joy, serenity and fulfillment, one day at a time.

For more information, call or write: **COSA** (Co-dependents of Sexual Addiction) 9337-B Katy Freeway Suite 142
Houston, TX 77024 (612) 537-6904

This and other organizations offer support to the spouse of a sexual addict. Support groups are available. The groups respect members' anonymity.

For more information, contact The National Council on Sexual Addiction and Compulsivity , at (770) 989-9754 or at the website: www.ncsac.org

APPENDIX 5

The Grief Process

As a spouse of a sexual addict, you are bound to experience loss. You will suffer through the grief process, much like anyone else who had lost a loved one. The difference is that you have lost a relationship while your loved one is still alive. You experience the death of your marriage as you knew it. You lose your ability to trust. If you allow yourself to journey through these stages, you will emerge as a whole person again. If you get stuck in one of the stages and cannot move forward, you may need professional help to do so. Allow yourself months of time to move through all of these stages.

Stage One: Denial and Isolation
Your husband is not who you thought he was and you cannot believe this is happening to you. Yet you are too ashamed and embarrassed to consider seeking the comfort of others.

Stage Two: **Anger**
You perceived reality wrongly and were easily deceived. You experience a profound loss of trust and security.

Expect six weeks to six months of rage, anger and resentment. You are angry at the whole world as you try to answer the question "Why me?" Anger is necessary to help you temporarily disassociate from your mate.

Stage Three: **Bargaining**
You experience excessive guilt and wish for some sort of punishment for not having seen what was coming. Or you expect some sort of prize for your own "good behavior." If only I did this, then…or if only I do that,then… but the bargaining does not take the pain away or clean up the mess created by the addiction(s).

Stage Four: Sadness/Depression

You finally allow yourself to feel, in all of its entirety, the great sense of loss. Your depression is reactive to a critical event and necessary to prepare you to possibly leave a very meaningful relationship. Your friends will help you through this stage with their encouragement and reassurances. You must be allowed to go through this sadness without feeling forced to look at the sunny side of things. You will need to examine the dark side of life for a long period of time.

Stage Five: Acceptance

You may not necessarily feel happy and you may almost feel void of feelings. At this stage you are integrating that you and your spouse have experienced a traumatic event in your married life. The addiction(s) are real and have caused pain in your lives. Yet the struggle is over. You both are now ready to boldly continue the recovery journey.

The stages of the grief process are adapted from those outlined by Elisabeth Kubler-Ross, M.D., author of *On Death and Dying,* copyright 1969, published by Macmillan Publishing Co., Inc. The author is unaware of the above interpretations, as applied to sex addiction.

APPENDIX 6

Sexual Addiction

According to the National Council on Sexual Addiction and Compulsivity (NCSAC), **sex addicts** are defined as persons who "engage in persistent and escalating patterns of sexual behaviors acted out despite increasing negative consequences to self or others." **Sex offenders** are defined as persons who "engage in illegal sexual behaviors involving victimization, and often demonstrating addictive elements and patterns in their sexual acting out."

Addictive Sexual Behaviors May Include:
- Compulsive Masturbation
- Multiple Affairs
- Consistent Use of Pornography
- Unsafe Sex
- Sexual Anorexia
- Multiple or Anonymous Partners
- Phone, Cybersex
- Strip Clubs and Adult Bookstores
- Prostitution

Offending Sexual Behaviors May Include:
- Exhibitionism
- Voyeurism
- Child Pornography
- Pedophilia
- Stalking
- Sexual Harassment
- Professional Misconduct **Consequences Include:**
- Social
- Relationship

- Emotional
- Legal
- Physical
- Financial

More information is available at (770) 989-9754 or using the websites: www.ncsac.org

APPENDIX 7

Manic-Depression or Substance-Induced Mood Disorder ?

According to the DSM IV Manual, a "Manic Episode" is defined to be: a distinct period during which there is an abnormally and persistently elevated, expansive, or irritable mood. The mood disturbance must be accompanied by at least three additional symptoms from a list that includes inflated self-esteem or grandiosity, decreased need for sleep, pressure of speech, flight of ideas, distractibility, increased involvement in goal-directed activities with a high potential for painful consequences. Increased sexual drive, fantasies, and behavior are often present. Symptoms include excessive involvement in pleasurable activities that may include but are not limited to: unrestrained buying sprees, sexual indiscretions or foolish business investments. Manic Episodes typically begin suddenly, with a rapid escalation of symptoms over a few days. Frequently, Manic Episodes occur following psychosocial stressors. The episodes usually last from a few weeks to several months and are briefer and end more abruptly than
Major Depressive Episodes. In many instances (50%-60%) a Major Depressive Episode immediately precedes or immediately follows a Manic Episode.

Contrast the above definition of "Manic Episode" with the following definition of a "Substance-Induced Mood Disorder":

The essential feature of Substance-Induced Mood disorder is a prominent and persistent disturbance in mood that is judged to be due to the direct physiological effects of a substance. Depending on the nature of the substance and the context in which the symptoms occur, the disturbance may involve depressed mood or markedly diminished interest or pleasure or elevated, expansive, or irritable mood.

A substance (such as alcohol, amphetamines, cocaine, hallucinogens, inhalants, opiates or others) is judged to be etiologically related to the mood disturbance. Symptoms like those seen in a Manic Episode may be precipitated by a drug of abuse. The symptoms cause clinically significant distress or impairment in social, occupational, or other important areas of functioning, in excess of what would be expected given the type or amount of the substance used or the duration of use.

Some medications or somatic treatments for depression (e.g. electroconvulsive therapy or light therapy) can also induce manic-like mood disturbances.

APPENDIX 8

Recovering Couples Anonymous

According to a position paper published by the National Council on Sexual Addiction and Compulsivity (NCSAC):

Sexual addiction is a family disease. Both partners have been part of the problem and both must be willing to participate in the recovery process, individually and together. Couples who are willing to identify and to work through individual issues such as family or origin difficulties, possible past traumas or neglect, and the need for better skills to cultivate intimacy, can do well in recovery. Couples who do well (1) have made their individual recovery a first priority, (2) both connect with others through attending 12step meetings as well as reach out to others for support, (3) usually have individual and couple counseling to identify systems that no longer work, (4) accept that couple recovery is a challenging and evolving journey, (5) read books and employ audiovisual resources for information, (6) are willing to grow spiritually and, (7) have a strong respect for and commitment toward each other.

WHAT TO EXPECT: The first three to six months of couple recovery are usually the most stressful. Both partners will experience a wide range of powerful feelings. There are often difficulties in the areas of communication styles, intimacy levels, sexuality, spirituality, parenting, past trauma, and finances. Identification of the sexual addiction/co-addiction systems, although painful at first, holds hope for eventual relief of the far greater pain of the addiction. The following is a list of what to expect in the early stages:

Relief: The addict usually finds a great sense of relief after admitting the secret of the addiction. The end of the double life and shame may bring a premature sense of accomplishment which needs to be reinforced by attending meetings, going to therapy, and connecting with program friends for support. Co-addicts also feel a sense of relief at the end of secrecy and validation of their experience of pain.

Anger: Both partners can expect to experience anger. The revelation that the life partner is a sex addict may trigger much anger mixed with legitimate hurt and betrayal. The addict feels anger about the need to make changes as part of recovery. Both partners may blame and shame the other.

Hope: The work being done by both partners can bring new life and hope to the relationship. Both partners are encouraged to attend separate 12step meetings as well as couples meetings such as Recovering Couples Anonymous.

Self-esteem: The self-esteem of both partners initially may worsen but with continued recovery will improve as both work a recovery program.

Intimacy: Recovering couples begin to communicate at a more intimate level, often on issues they have never discussed before. Communication skills such as empathic listening, being respectful, and expressing vulnerability, are essential to both partners' recovery.

Grief: The addict experiences pain over the loss of their "best friend," the addiction. The co-addict mourns the loss of the relationship as it was imagined to be, the reality of the partner being a sex addict. Co-addicts often berate themselves for not having been aware sooner of the addiction.

Sexual issues: Sexuality has a different meaning in recovery. The goal becomes intimacy rather than intensity. Abstinence, and later the frequency, types and quality of sexual contacts, are issues that the recovering couple must address. Past sexual relationships as well as possible past child sexual abuse of either partner need to be explored. Where other sexual partners were involved, the possibility of HIV infection and other sexually transmitted diseases must be faced early. Couples who continue to learn about healthy sexuality will do better as they address these sexual issues.

Spirituality: Couples who grow spiritually together have hope that a power greater than themselves is also involved in the re-creating of their relationship.

HOW TO GET HELP: A therapist trained in sexual addiction is an invaluable recovery tool for both the individual and for the relationship. Some addicts and co-addicts benefit from intensive outpatient services or possibly inpatient treatment. For information on such services, write or call the National Council on Sexual Addiction and Compulsivity.

Rev. 9/96

Telephone counseling appointments with Dr. Douglas Weiss, a sexual addiction recovery professional, are also available by calling (817) 3774278.

There is a counseling fee involved.

APPENDIX 9

Pornography

According to the National Coalition for the Protection of Children and Families (NCPCF):

Fact #1: Hard-core pornography is prosecutable and child pornography is illegal. Although it objectifies women and influences the way they are viewed by men, soft-core pornography is in an entirely different category from hard-core pornography. Types of illegal pornography include women engaging in sex acts with animals; women being tortured and mutilated as well as defecated and urinated upon for sexual pleasure. Child pornography shows nude children and sex between adults and children, some as young as six months old. The Supreme Court has ruled that these materials are not protected by the First Amendment. Therefore, responsible citizens have the right to see laws that limit the availability of illegal pornography enacted and enforced. That is not censorship—which is prior restraint by the government. It is common sense.

Fact #2: Pornography harms people. Hard-core, child pornography and even soft-core pornography are not harmless forms of entertainment. They degrade and abuse the women and children who appear in such materials as well as those who view it. Child pornography is a permanent record of child sexual abuse. In addition, studies indicate that these materials have a tremendous negative influence on the attitudes and behaviors of people who consume them. Land use studies indicate that sexually-oriented businesses encourage prostitution, increase sexual assaults and attract other criminal activity.

Fact #3: Illegal pornography is pervasive, influential and addictive. To deny the power of pornography is to deny the power of advertising. Thousands of video stores provide hard-core pornography. In addition, technological advances are being exploited by pornographers who transmit millions of hard-core pornographic images via the computer. Studies say that boys ages 12-17 are among the primary consumers of pornography.

Their attitudes toward sex, marriage, family and women are profoundly influenced by what they see and read. Pornographers know this and target these young men.

Why the man you love uses porn:

Out of curiosity, males are naturally drawn to pornography. Pornography is an aid to masturbation, which provides sexual gratification without intimacy. But men don't use pornography just because it's sexually stimulating.

Other reasons are…

- Pornography provides relief from pain often caused by childhood neglect, abuse, family dysfunction or some childhood trauma
- Poor coping mechanisms—masturbation is a stress reducer
- Fantasy involved in porn/masturbation provides escape from reality
- Society conditioning that being actively sexual is the social "norm"
- False understanding of intimate relationships: relationship with porn carries no risk of rejection
- Fear of intimacy
- Fear of rejection
- Need for validation of masculinity

When confronted or caught, his reactions may range from denial and anger to blame/guilt and hurt. He may try to play down your concerns or completely ignore you. Use this time to determine his stance on his porn use.

His position will likely be one of these three.

Lawlessness

He has no sense of a problem:

"I know pornography is wrong. I don't care that it's wrong. I want to use it."

He feels honesty makes his behavior OK. The honest approach of this stance is hopeful.

Minimization

He makes the problem smaller than it is, owning a percentage of the problem but denies its magnitude with rationalization: "It's not as bad as you think. It's a hobby."

They value an image of goodness rather than having qualities that make them good.

Confession

A confessor is a broken man who has given up trying to be good. He admits his porn use has caused harm:

"My human relationships have suffered because of my life of porn, fantasy and self-gratification."

This man wants to recover and needs your help.

The most vital ingredient for recovery is to seek counseling, both as a couple and individually. For successful recovery, set guidelines from which to build a healthy relationship. These "boundaries" are set by you. Soliciting the advice of a counselor beforehand and during recovery will help you better understand yourself and the relationship.

For more information about a counselor near you, contact the National Coalition referral service at (513) 521-6227 or visit their website at: www.nationalcoalition.org

APPENDIX 10

Dysfunctional Families

John Friel and Linda Friel are two experts in the field of dysfunctional family systems. According to these authors, adults who have grown up in dysfunctional family systems often exhibit emotional, psychological and physical symptoms, which may include some of the following:

Emotional/Psychological
1. Depression
2. Anxiety/panic attacks
3. Suicide or suicidal thoughts
4. Obsessions and compulsions
5. Chemical addictions
6. Low self-esteem
7. Personality disorders
8. Phobias
9. Hysteria
10. Sexual dysfunction
11. Suspiciousness
12. Intimacy problems
13. Dissociation
14. Flat affect
15. Difficulty concentrating
16. Excessive anger
17. Low frustration tolerance
18. Passive/aggressive personality
19. Extreme dependency
20. Inability to be interdependent
21. Inability to play or have fun
22. Inability to be assertive
23. People-pleasing

24. Approval seeking
25. Identity confusion

Physical
1. Chemical dependency
2. Eating disorders
3. Accident proneness/chronic pain syndrome
4. Tension and migraine headaches
5. Respiratory problems
6. Ulcers, colitis, digestive problems
7. Constipation/diarrhea
8. Sleep disorders
9. Muscle tension
10. TMJ (Temporomandibular Joint Disorder)

Characteristics of a healthy family system:
1. The family system provides maintenance functions such as food, clothing and shelter.
2. The family should also provide safety, warmth and nurturanceto its members.
3. Each family is provided a sense of love and belonging.
4. Each family member also experiences autonomy and separateness, including privacy and uniqueness.
5. Families function to promote self-esteem or a sense of worth ineach family member, encouraging personal dignity and value.
6. Healthy family systems get to make mistakes, with room forhuman error and imperfection.
7. Families get to have fun through silly, playful, and creativeactivities.
8. Families have spirituality by developing a relationship with creation, nature, a Higher Power or cosmos or however they may explain it.

The needs and functions listed above are things that each family member should be getting. In a dysfunctional family, those functions are often divided up separately and delegated to one specific family member in the form of relatively rigid roles.

Characteristics of an unhealthy family system:
1. Physical, emotional or sexual abuse/neglect and vicarious abuse(awareness of some other family member being abused)
2. Perfectionism
3. Rigid rules, lifestyle and/or belief systems
4. The "No Talk Rule"/Keeping "The Family Secrets"
5. Inability to identify and/or express feelings
6. Triangulation (a communication pattern using one person as anintermediary)
7. Double messages/double binds ("I love you/go away." or "Surewe like you/why can't you be more like your brother?")
8. Inability to play, have fun and be spontaneous
9. High tolerance for inappropriate behavior/pain
10. Enmeshment (My problems become your problems and your problems become my problems.)

Growing up in a dysfunctional family system leads to identity problems, trust problems, intimacy problems, and co-dependency problems.

Healing is a process which should include identification of the problems, professional help, a 12-step program and spiritual growth.

Note: The information found in Appendix 10 is a summary of the information shared in the book, Adult Children: The Secrets of *Dysfunctional Families*, by John and Linda Friel, published in 1988 by Health Communications, Inc.

References/Bibliography

Amodeo, John, Ph.D. (1994). **Love & Betrayal.** New York, N.Y. Ballantine Books. This book takes an in-depth look at the loss of trust in intimate relationships and how to rebuild a sense of trust in oneself and others.

Courage to Change: One Day at a Time in AL-ANON II. ALANON Family Group Headquarters, Inc. 1992. This small book is a daily reading guide for persons in relationship with an addictive personality or persons who grew up in the home of an addict.

Carnes, Patrick, Ph.D. (1989) **Contrary to Love.** Center City, Minnesota: Hazelden Educational Materials. This book will help persons to understand the addictive system, the co-addiction traits of the family and the recovery process.

Carnes, Patrick, Ph.D. (1992) **Out of the Shadows** (Second Edition). Center City, Minnesota: Hazelden. This book pioneered the study and understanding of sexual addiction.

Dayton, Tian, Ph.D. (1992) **Forgiving and Moving On.** Deerfield Beach, Florida: Health Communication, Inc. This book provides daily affirmations and inspirational messages for personal change.

Friel, John and Friel, Linda. (1988) **Adult Children: The Secrets of Dysfunctional Families.** Deerfield Beach, Florida: Health Communications, Inc. This book will meticulously explore the family system and its impact upon individual family members.

Hall, Laurie. (1996) **An Affair of the Mind.** Wheaton, IL: Tyndale House Publishers. This book takes a poignant look at a woman's battle to salvage her family from the effects of pornography and sexual addiction. Milkman, Harvey and Sunderwirth, Stanley. (1987) **Craving for Ecstasy.** San Francisco, CA: Jossey-Bass Inc. This book takes an in-depth look at pleasure-seeking behaviors and how our passions can become addictions. Weiss, Douglass, Ph.D. (1998) **The Final Freedom.** Fort Worth, Texas: Discovery Press. This book provides a better understanding of what sexual addiction is and the steps toward recovery.

Other Helpful Resources:

For certified sexual addiction therapists in your city, call The Meadows at 1.800.632.3697.

Helpful Websites: www.hazelden.org This site connects you with the Hazelden

Foundation, which is a not-for-profit organization that promotes treatment and understanding of chemical dependency. www.integrityonline.com This site will give you information about an online filtering system, to help filter out offensive material from the World Wide Web. www.iUniverse.com An internet book publishing company which will connect you with worldwide books and publications. www.ncsac.org This site has valuable information for persons seeking recent articles about sexual addiction/sexual compulsion. www.sexaddict.com This site will connect you with the Heart to Heart Counseling Center. It is loaded with additional resources and the opportunity to set up a telephone counseling session with Dr. Douglas Weiss.

End Notes

1. See Appendix 1
2. See Appendix 1
3. See Appendix 2
4. See Appendix 4
5. See Appendix 5
6. See Appendix 6
7. See Appendix 6
8. See Appendix 3
9. See Appendix 1
10. See Appendix 7
11. See Appendix 8
12. See Appendix 9
13. See Appendix 10
14. See Appendix 10

The US Review of Books

Love Over Lust: How Love Overcame the Power of Addiction
by Karen Valiant
Reviewed by Rebecca L. Morgan

"I felt like I was grieving and, in fact, I was. A certain innocence was gone."

In this candid memoir of betrayal and humiliation, the author reveals how she uncovered her husband's alcohol and sexual addictions that jeopardized the fate of her fourteen-year marriage and sent her spiraling into turmoil. This story is her journey to heal and forgive after discovering her husband's numerous indiscretions that unraveled the life she believed she was living and exposed the reality of a relationship with an addict. Describing the bevy of emotions one experiences when confronting a family member's addiction, the author details her own path to recovery achieved by gaining an understanding of the psychological effects associated with substance abuse and compulsive behavior. Committed to preserving her second marriage, she strives to overcome her devastation and shame with the intent of regaining her lost integrity. Through her faith, she unearths the healing power of forgiveness and releases her fear of deception to trust once again.

In concise, chronological chapters, the author explores the nature of secrets and questions how well we can truly know another, even our mate. Her research on the subject of addictive behavior is cited throughout her story, including references to psychiatrists and organizations from which she garnered beneficial information. While some readers may find the author's willingness to disclose intimate details of her spouse's unfaithful actions disconcerting, she routinely states that her desire for sharing her personal story is to assist others who find themselves in similar situations but are embarrassed to seek support. The integral theme of the story is love and one couple's ability to repair their shattered relationship, but the author strongly emphasizes the importance of professional counseling for both the addict and family members in the recovery process.

www.ingramcontent.com/pod-product-compliance
Lightning Source LLC
LaVergne TN
LVHW040154080526
838202LV00042B/3156